NUR

CW00706641

When Ward Sister Zena Foster falls in love with one of her patients, a wealthy young Arab businessman, she decides to work in a hospital in Kuwait for a year before making up her mind to accept his marriage proposal. But the attractive neuro-surgeon, Theodore Smythe, seems determined to thwart her plans . . .

NURSE FOSTER

BY

RHONA UREN

MILLS & BOON LIMITED
London · Sydney · Toronto

First published in Great Britain 1980
by Robert Hale Limited, Clerkenwell House,
Clerkenwell Green, London EC1R 0HT

This edition published 1982 by Mills & Boon Limited,
15–16 Brook's Mews, London W1A 1DR

ISBN 0 263 73924 4

03/0782

Set in 10 on 10½ pt Linotron Times

Photoset by Rowland Phototypesetting Ltd
Bury St Edmunds, Suffolk
Made and printed in Great Britain by
Richard Clay (The Chaucer Press) Ltd
Bungay, Suffolk

CHAPTER ONE

ZENA sat at a corner table in her favourite Knightsbridge restaurant. She had finished her toasted tea-cake and slice of chocolate gateau, had drunk her second cup of tea and now it was time for her to leave. She was of medium height and slimly built. She had a pale, almost white complexion and fair hair which was nearer to silver in colour than gold. She could have been too colourless had it not been for her deep blue eyes which were round like a kitten's, edged with thick dark lashes.

She signalled to the waitress who came across to her walking laboriously on flat feet. 'Are you on duty again tonight, Sister?' she asked as she made out the bill.

'No, I'm not on again until the morning, thank goodness. And how are you keeping?'

'Mustn't grumble, dear, if it wasn't for me legs I'd be fine. It's all this standing around that's the trouble. My veins want seeing to, I shouldn't wonder.' She collected the coins that Zena left for her and stacked the dishes.

'You ought to get your doctor to have a look at them; now mind you do,' Zena said with a smile and made her way slowly over the pink carpeted floor to the lifts.

Out in the street she stood for a moment enjoying the feel of the early spring breeze, and the casual comfort of slacks and sweater in place of her uniform dress and apron. The sun was shining and she decided to take a walk in the park. As she waited for the lights to change so that she could cross the road she saw, on a newstand, the headline, MAN SHOT IN EDGWAREBURY BANK RAID. With sudden interest she bought a paper and tucked it under her arm, then crossed into the park and sat on a bench to read all about it. She had expected to find it on the front page but could see no mention of it. There was: 'Tragic death of mother of five as fire sweeps

5

flat', 'Unemployed man wins jackpot with his one pre-
mium bond', 'Police combing Dartmoor for missing
child', 'Pop star weds for sixth time'. Details of the bank
raid had most probably appeared in a mid-day edition of
the paper. She read for a while, watched the pigeons and
sparrows greedily searching for crumbs, then as the
breeze grew colder she zipped up her anorak and decided to go window-shopping. As she folded the news-
paper she saw in the stop press: 'BANK RAID MAN
OPERATED ON IN EDGWAREBURY HOSPITAL.
CONDITION SATISFACTORY'.

Edgwarebury Hospital! That meant that he would be
in her ward, for she was in charge of both men's and
women's surgical wards. Although she still had several
hours to go before she had intended to return to
Edgwarebury there was only one place she wanted to be
and that was in the hospital to make sure that all was
going well.

As the train rumbled along the Underground she
wondered who would have performed the operation.
Their top surgeon, Mr Moore, was on holiday in Elba,
which meant that it would have been either Dr Owens
the Registrar, or Dr Rosewood the Houseman. Staff-
nurse Penn was in charge of her wards. She was a very
able nurse but not an ideal person to be in control; she
was too happy-go-lucky. Then there was Nurse Wilson
in her second year who was reliable. Oh yes, there were
several good nurses as well as those from the Agency,
and the newcomer, Nurse Simmons.

The hospital was within walking distance of the station
and she could see it long before she reached the grounds.
It was an unprepossessing red brick building, its façade
darkening over the years, chiefly from the dust and
fumes belched out by the traffic which flowed con-
tinuously along the busy roadway which ran in front of
the hospital, from the Marble Arch to outer northern
suburbia. Newer, but no less ugly structures practically
filled the grounds; the blood bank, the chest clinic,
laboratories, the forensic block and the stores. Reached

by a covered arcade when the weather was bad were the hostels and the canteen.

Zena followed the path which led to the ambulance station, through the Casualty Department and along interminable corridors, until she came once again into the open with gravel paths laid between lawns which led eventually to the nurses' hostel.

She still had an immense feeling of pride as she by-passed the corridor on which were the nurses' quarters, and went instead to the sisters' separate flatlets. This had become her ambition, to become a sister. To that end she had spent her spare time studying for examinations, and working anti-social hours. She had allowed any chance of romance to pass her by with scarcely a glance; had never had a regular boy-friend, considering them time-wasters, and as people who could come between you and your dreams. Now, at twenty-six, she sometimes wondered with a chilly feeling around her heart, whether in attaining her ambition she had lost something infinitely more precious, the chance of having a husband and family of her own.

Her flatlet consisted of a bed-sitting room, a cupboard-sized kitchen, a built-in shower and a wash-basin hidden by a curtain on rails, with, next to it, a gas ring. There was a communal bathroom at the end of the block which was for the use of all the sisters. Zena showered and changed into her uniform, for although she was not on duty and would be merely visting her ward she considered it essential to her status, and better for discipline, to look the part. She was pleased with the new issue dress and small shoulder cape which was the same blue as her eyes and well-tailored to fit her slender figure. She twisted her hair into a knot in the nape of her neck and pinned on her freshly pleated hat. She applied a little discreet make-up to her eyes and lips, firmly of the opinion that it did the patients good to see you looking your best and encouraged them to do the same as soon as they felt able.

The afternoon visitors had long since left and prepara-

tions would be in hand for the evening meal and yet
another batch of visitors. As Zena passed her office door
she saw that the room was empty, so went on to the
women's ward. Beds were curtained off where patients
who were bed-ridden were either washing themselves or
being washed. Others in a uniform of quilted housecoats
shuffled along on their be-slippered feet to chat together
while they awaited their turn to go to the bathroom.
Bunches of flowers and bags of fruit lay on bedside
lockers until such time as the ancillary workers were able
to transfer them to bowls and vases.

Staff-nurse Penn, a stocky ginger-haired girl, was
adjusting a saline drip over a patient in a bed in the far
corner of the ward. Zena crossed over to her, nodding a
greeting to some of the patients as she passed. Sue Penn
glanced up at the drip with an air of concentration then
smiled reassuringly at her patient and said a few words.

'Staff,' Zena said as she paused behind her.

Sue spun round, the blood rose in her face and
involuntarily her fists tightened. 'Hello Sister, you aren't
due back this evening,' she said with a smile which did
not quite hide her annoyance.

Zena unhooked the chart from the end of the bed and
studied it for a moment. Then she looked at the temperature chart on the wall. 'That is fluctuating quite a bit.
Has she any problems?'

Sue moved closer and said in a low voice, 'Yes, she is
complaining of abdominal pain.'

Zena transferred her gaze to the patient. 'Hello, Mrs
Day, what's this I hear about a pain?'

Tears of weakness filled the woman's eyes as she
moved her head restlessly on the pillow. 'I . . . I feel
awful,' she whimpered.

Zena nodded. 'Where is the pain?'

The woman pointed to the area of her wound. 'It hurts
me dreadfully if I move. I keep wanting to cough and I'm
afraid to.'

Zena replaced the chart on the bed. 'Yes, I see. Of
course it is early days yet and it is bound to feel sore.' She

turned to Sue. 'Have a word with the doctor, Staff, and see if he will prescribe something that will help to ease the pain. And when you have finished in here I would like to see you in my office, please.'

Away from the ward the difference in their status was ignored for Zena and Sue were the same age and had come to Edgwarebury Hospital within a few months of each other and were firm friends. Sue hooked a chair with her foot and flopped down in it opposite Zena. 'So how's Knightsbridge? Did you spend your month's salary?'

'That, my dear Sue, would go nowhere up there. With a bit of luck it might just stretch to one of their less expensive sweaters.'

'How the other half lives!' Sue sighed.

'I just browse . . . and admire . . . and envy, oh lots and lots of envy . . . then I have lunch and tea guaranteed to put inches on a greedy girl's waistline. Does it show?' She stared apprehensively at her belt.

She threw back her head and laughed. 'You should worry! Wait until you are my size.' She levelled an accusing glance in Zena's direction. 'Why have you come in? Didn't you trust me to cope?'

'Don't be daft, love; it is my ward and when I saw on the hoardings that a man shot in an Edgwarebury bank raid had been operated on here, well I just had to get back. Tell me about it.'

She tucked a wisp of ginger hair behind her ear. 'Trust you to want to know the gory details!'

'No, I want to know how he's doing. Who operated?'

'He is doing all right. As to who operated, I'll tell you that in a minute. First of all . . .' She hummed the signature tune of a television thriller. 'It is soon after opening time in the bank. Customers are queuing at the counters. Suddenly . . . drama! Three men wearing hideous masks burst in. "Your money, chums, hand it over," one of them says. The chap at the counter says "Scram and stop acting the goat!" At which the raiders turn real nasty and whoops! Before their very eyes these blokes produce guns.' Sue laughed joyfully. 'I'd like to have seen their faces.'

'You mean behind the masks?'

'No, fathead, the staff behind the counter, and the customers. Well, to continue. Just at that moment the doors are pushed open and in walks our hero. Without saying a word his very presence scares the daylights out of our villians. One of them has a nervous twitch and his gun goes off. He wasn't aiming at anyone apparently, but the shot ricocheted and hit our hero in the head. And if that wasn't rotten luck I don't know what you'd call it.'

'Poor chap! Still he might have been killed, I suppose. You say he was shot in the head?'

'Yes and very nasty it was too. When Dr Owen saw the pictures he didn't much like what he saw. You've got to hand it to him; it couldn't have been easy for him to admit that he didn't feel capable of doing the op well enough.'

'No, I suppose not, but what else could he do? So what happened?'

'Well, Miss Simms got on to St Stephen's and they sent down a consultant neuro-surgeon, a Mr Theodore Smythe, very posh, given the red carpet treatment. Anyhow, he apparently did a darn good job, at least that's what everybody says,' Sue explained.

'Thank goodness for that. Of course it would have to happen while Mr Moore was away.' And when I was away, too, she thought. 'Where have you put him?'

'In the side ward that Mr Griffiths had. Is that okay?'

Zena nodded her approval. 'Yes, of course, that's fine. He'll need the quiet.'

'You call it quiet there?' Sue exploded. 'It's right opposite the kitchen you may remember, and patients are complaining all the time about the noise in there. They swear that the night staff play football with the saucepans while others shout out over the din intimate details of their love-life.'

Zena's face became expressionless; she had heard it

all before. 'Sound is always magnified at night. Those patients who complain can have sleeping pills if they wish. I will write it on their charts.' She pushed her chair away and rose to her feet. 'Thanks, Sue. Now you had better be getting back to the ward; I'm sure it is more than time for the medicine round. I will go and have a look at the new patient.'

The side ward was a small dim room whose windows looked out on to roofs and chimneys. In addition to the bedside locker there were a scuffed wooden wardrobe and chest of drawers. Zena looked at the man asleep in the bed with a feeling of alarm. Against the whiteness of his pillow and the bandages which covered his eyes and his head the small area of face visible was a greyish-yellow. Instinctively she felt for his pulse while her eyes checked that his drip was functioning. She took his chart from the end of the bed and reading that his name was Sami Gharbally felt an immense relief that the colour of his skin was not entirely due to his condition. His age was put at approximately thirty. As she was replacing the chart she heard someone entering the room. She swung around angrily to see a tall man of about the same age as the patient, with the build of a Rugby player or possibly a policeman. He had a square jaw which gave him a ruthless look accentuated by the steel grey of his eyes. His hair was thick, straight and light brown.

Zena moved swiftly to bar his way in. 'You have no right to be here,' she said authoritatively. 'Kindly go outside immediately.'

The intruder tossed a strand of hair off his forehead, and stared at her coolly, but made no move to obey her.

'My patient is in no condition to have visitors, neither can he answer any questions. If you ring the hospital in the morning you will be told when, and if, you will be permitted to see him.' She placed her hand on the door to usher him outside.

The man's eyes narrowed. '*Your* patient? On the contrary he is *my* patient. I don't recall seeing you before. And now if you will kindly stand aside I wish to take a look at him.'

Zena flushed crimson, the unaccustomed colour making her eyes sparkle. 'Is it . . . is it Mr Smythe? I do beg your pardon, sir; I thought you were from the press or the police.' She moved to make way for him. 'My name is Foster. Sister Foster,' she said apologetically.

He gave her a casual nod as he went over to the patient.

'Are you satisfied with his condition, sir?' she asked, noticing the frown on his face.

'To the extent that he is still breathing, yes.'

'Is there likely to be any permanent damage, sir?'

'I have no idea,' he said shortly.

Nurse Simmons hurriedly entered the room. Then, seeing that Mr Smythe was already there, stopped awkwardly. His eyes softened and creased in a smile. 'Ah, I see my patient is in good hands. You've come to do a check on him, is that right?'

'Yes sir, half-hourly observations, sir,' she murmured.

'Good. Well, we will see what they say, shall we?'

As they waited Zena surreptitiously studied the surgeon's face; noticed the lines of weariness around his eyes, his eyebrows so much darker than his hair, and his mouth—well-shaped but cruelly tight at the corners.

When Nurse Simmons had completed the tests he compared the figures with those already on the chart and nodded. 'Thank you, nurse, do they seem satisfactory to you?'

'Yes sir,' she whispered.

'Good. And I think so too. Now, I shall be staying the night here in the hospital in case I am needed, if you will be so good as to inform the night sister, please.' He smiled at her again and with a last minute brief nod in Zena's direction walked swiftly from the room.

Rage and humiliation swept through her, tautening every nerve. Never since she had obtained her promotion had she felt so unimportant—as if she were a mere junior, instead of the competent sister she knew herself to be. No, not even a junior, she reminded herself, for he had smiled at Nurse Simmons, and even asked for her opinion, whereas he had practically ignored her own presence.

With her head held high, her feet tap-tapped determinedly along the corridor. There was a sound of rattling dishes in the kitchen and water gurgling in the sluice. There was coughing and talk and laughter in the wards, and as she reached her office she saw, through the partly opened door, Dr Rosewood perched on the corner of her desk chatting to Sue. She stopped abruptly, tingling with indignation. That was *her* desk he was making free with! She moved forward, then stopped and her anger fell away leaving her with a feeling of disorientation. Today, as far as the hospital and the staff were concerned she was nobody, for she was off-duty and Sue Penn reigned supreme. As far as Mr Theodore Smythe was concerned she did not even exist, for she had not been there when he arrived, nor when he operated; neither had she admitted the new patient to her ward. His dealings had been with the staff who were on duty, who would, in the fullness of time, pass any information to her. Now if Mr Moore had performed the operation he would have discussed it with her and told her all the details, whether she was on duty or not. But this Mr Smythe apparently acted strictly according to the book, and was not a very pleasant man.

As she made her way back to her flat she wished that she had not visited her ward, for Sue had not been pleased, either. It was not nice being made to feel like an intruder and she wished that she had not chosen to take this particular day off.

She filled her kettle to make a pot of tea, then switched on her small television which was a present to herself. Normally she would go along to the communal lounge but tonight she wanted to be alone. She had letters to write, a good book to read and small articles of clothing to wash. But she could not settle to anything.

She switched off the television which was showing a
repeat of a programme which she had not enjoyed the
first time round. She went over to her desk and picked up
a photograph she had taken on a trip home. It featured
her mother and father standing in their garden against a
background of huge bushes of rhododendrons. They
were sunburnt and smiling, and for a moment she felt a
longing to be back with them in the little Cornish town
where she had lived and gone to school. She replaced the
picture and took from the drawer her writing pad and the
last letter she had received from her mother, intending
to reply to it. She read it through, noting with only vague
interest items of news about people she either had never
known or remembered but slightly. She wrote her
address and glanced at the calendar to check the date.
She pressed her pen open and shut as she searched her
mind in vain for something that might interest her
parents, but it was no use. Any letter that she managed
to write tonight would not be worth reading.

She went to the sink and washed out a few things,
thinking as she did so of her day in Knightsbridge; of the
out-of-her-world dresses and lingerie, shoes and furs,
fine china and exquisite silver-ware, to say nothing of the
luxury foods, and she wondered what it would be like to
be one of the wealthy women who regularly did their
shopping there. When she had hung her washing on the
small line she had rigged up, she walked over to the
window where the sound of scrunching gravel on the
paths below told her it was visiting time again. And there
they were, all the good and loyal friends and relatives of
the patients, giving up their time to bring flowers and
fruit and a little brightness into the regimentation and
discomfort of hospital life.

Hospital life! She suddenly felt a great dislike of it, of
the drips and injections, of dressings and medicine
trolleys and bed-pans. The atmosphere which normally
exhilarated her now depressed her, and she knew perfectly well why that was. It was Mr Smythe with his cool
snubbing eyes who had caused the change by reducing

her to nothing. Impatiently she willed herself to blot the picture of him from her mind, and settled down to read her book, but there he was, on every page, staring up at her with empty eyes. 'To hell with him!' she said aloud, flinging her book aside. She looked at her watch and saw that it was still some hours before she could sensibly go to bed. Deciding that she would be foolish to sit here with the ghost of an unfriendly stranger, she put on her cape and made her way to the canteen to search more for pleasant company than for food.

CHAPTER TWO

BY the following morning when she was on duty again, Zena felt her normal self and looked forward to the day's work ahead. She read the night nurse's report and saw that the men's ward had been quiet except for an emergency admittance at 2.50 a.m. when Simon Cotton had been sent up from Casualty after a haemorrhageing. Sami Gharbally's condition had stabilised and was satisfactory. In the women's ward, Mrs Day had slept badly and still complained of pain. Mrs Bottome was unable to sleep, had refused a sleeping pill and had been given hot milk at 3.30 a.m. Mrs Yip had been found by a porter wandering in the entrance hall, and became very excitable and screamed when he attempted to take her back to the ward. Mrs Cooke had a persistent cough. It was the usual sort of report.

Zena turned to her stack of paperwork, a never-ending pile, and the telephone, which rang time and again, broke her concentration. When she was free to do her morning round of the wards, breakfast had long been cleared away and the cleaners were at work. Today was not an operating day but notices restricting food and liquid intake would be pinned over beds later on for those who were due in theatre the following morning.

Zena spoke a few words to each patient but moved fairly swiftly along the rows of beds until she came to someone in need of more attention. Mrs Bottome was a haggard-faced woman with discontented eyes and a petulant mouth. She had been admitted some weeks before with a ruptured spleen, caused by slipping on some oil in her bath and banging her side on the panelling. The doctors were satisfied with her condition but she complained constantly of minor discomforts and

Zena wondered whether they were real or imaginary.

'Good morning, Mrs Bottome, and how are you this morning?' she asked pleasantly.

'How am I? You may well ask,' the woman replied, plucking nervously at her lace bed-jacket. 'I should have thought a hospital should be a place of peace where a sick person can relax, but you ought to try and sleep here. Last night the racket was unbearable, with coughing and screaming and nurses shouting to each other and switching lights on and off. And the snoring! It was quite impossible to sleep.'

There was a stillness, a hush, as the patients in nearby beds listened to the conversation, wondering how she had the nerve to speak to Sister in such a way, guessing that she would get as good as she gave, and wanting to hear every word.

Zena seemed to grow an inch taller. 'This won't do, you know, Mrs Bottome. You have complained about sleeplessness before and were prescribed sleeping pills, but I understand you refused to take them. If the doctor thinks you need them then you must take them, you need your sleep. Now mind you take them tonight,' she said firmly, moving on to the next bed.

'Sleeping pills? I don't want them, I don't agree with them. You just shovel them down people's throats regardless. You ought to see that the nurses keep quiet. I don't want to hear a blow-by-blow account of their love life, shouted from the kitchen; I'm just not interested,' she said viciously.

Zena silently sympathised with her but knew there was little that could be done about it; staff was difficult to come by and easily offended. It was a sorry state of affairs but that was the way things were. But Mrs Bottome was an irritable woman and if she was not complaining about the noise it would be about something else. She moved back to her bed to study her chart. There seemed no reason why she should not be discharged. She would probably recover her health quicker at home; too much hospitalisation was bad for a person of her temperament. Zena decided to mention it to the doctor when he made his rounds.

A cleaner pushed a bed from the wall and plugged in the floor polisher.

'Switch that off, please,' Zena said authoritatively over the noise of the motor. 'Wait until I have finished in here or I can't hear myself speak.'

In the corner bed Mrs Day lay grey-faced and hollow-eyed and still complaining of pain, and Zena was thankful that Mr Moore would soon be back to keep an eye on her, as she feared there might be complications.

Mrs Yip was a tiny, slant-eyed young woman wearing an attractively patterned scarlet silk dressing-gown with a mandarin collar which made a pleasant splash of colour in the ward. 'Well, Mrs Yip, and what do you think you were doing last night? I hear you went walk-about. Where did you think you were going? Back to Japan?' Zena spoke severely but the corners of her mouth twitched.

'Oh Sister, it was so funnee,' she giggled, her eyes forming narrow gleaming slits. 'Do you know I thought I was in Hyde Park and I saw two of your policemen. I really saw them and I did not want them to catch me for I was in my nightgown, if you please! So I ran and ran and I screamed, oh so loud!'

'I wonder why? It could have been fun. Haven't you heard that our policemen are wonderful?' Zena joked.

The woman went on giggling. 'But it must have been a dream after all because the man who did catch me was not a policeman but a porter and I was not in Hyde Park but in this hospital. I have never had a dream so clear before and I did not like it.'

Zena patted her on the shoulder and made a mental note to mention to the doctor that the drug she had been prescribed perhaps should be changed.

She was entering her office when she came face to face with the tall and lanky Dr Owens. 'Ah Sister, just who I'm looking for. I am going to operate on Mr Cotton. He

was given his pre-med earlier on. Will you let them know
that I'll be using theatre one, please?'

As Zena was speaking on the telephone she saw Sue
passing the door and called over to her. She swung
around, her shoes squeaking on the tiled floor.

'Sister?' she said, bright and smiling as usual.

'Will you get Mr Cotton ready for theatre, please? Dr
Owens is operating immediately.'

Doing the round of the men's ward never took a great
deal of time. Those patients who were on the mend
seemed contented enough with a cigarette and the morning paper. The others appeared reconciled with their lot
and waited patiently for attention. Zena would never
subscribe to the generally expressed opinion that men
made worse patients tham women, for there was no
impatient complaining. Simon Cotton was already
under sedation and Sue and a porter were transferring
him to a trolley and a young nurse was preparing the bed
for his return.

Mr Hughes, wearing hospital issue pyjamas because
his elderly wife who suffered from arthritis in her hands
was unable to keep up with the washing, was busily
engaged with packets of coloured paper tissues and a
pair of scissors. Artificial carnations of all colours were
strewn over his bed and Zena paused to admire them.

'I tell you what I'll do, Sister,' he said, his old blue eyes
twinkling. 'The day you get married I'll make you the
finest bunch of carnations you've ever seen. Will you
carry them?'

Zena laughed. 'Come now, Mr Hughes, you can't fool
me. You will have forgotten that I ever existed long
before that day comes.'

He shook his grizzled grey head. 'I don't know, I'm
sure.'

'What don't you know, Mr Hughes?'

'I don't know what all the young men can be thinking
about, letting a lovely girl like you slip through their
fingers. If I was a younger man . . .' He raised his shaggy
eyebrows, then closed one eye in a salacious wink.

'Now that would be something like,' Zena grinned. 'But you know what it is, don't you? They don't make super men like you any more.'

She swung around as Pat O'Reilly walked towards the door.

'And where are you going?' she thundered.

'Just going to use the phone, Sister. Got to have a word with me old woman.'

Zena's eyes were quizzical. 'Oh yes, and what's her name today?'

'Eh?' There was a chorus of laughter and jeers from the men.

'Did you win anything yesterday?'

'Yesterday? Well no, I can't say that I did. But I'm on to a good one today. Would you like me to put a wee bit on for you?'

'No, thank you,' Zena said firmly. 'I've got better things to do with my money. Now please don't spend too long on the phone, there are other people who may want to use it. I've had complaints about you.'

Old Mr Willis, looking like a white-haired gnome, was ready with his daily joke. When Zena asked him how he felt he said he was fine apart from his corns which gave him jip, although he had had both legs amputated years ago.

The young man in the end bed wore head-phones and was obviously absorbed in the programme on the radio, so Zena looked at his chart, nodded to him and left the ward. In the side ward she saw Mr Gharbally moving restlessly on his pillow, so knew he was awake.

'Good morning, Mr Gharbally. I am Sister Foster in charge of this ward. I was not on duty yesterday when you were brought in but I know all about you. How do you feel this morning?'

His hands clenched into fists. 'Will you please tell me what happened?'

She moved closer to his bed. 'Tell me what you remember,' she said.

'Nothing. Just that I was shopping and . . . and then a

loud banging . . . an explosion that seemed to be right inside my head . . . Was it a bomb?' He spoke in a gentle, cultured voice.

'No it was not a bomb. First of all I'll tell you where you are. This is Edgwarebury Hospital.'

'Ah, I remember, I was in Edgwarebury. I needed some money, I think.'

'That's right, you had gone into a bank. What you didn't know was that a raid was going on and the men had guns. Whether it was by accident or on purpose, one of the guns went off. The men hadn't aimed it at anyone in particular, but the shot ricocheted from the top of the wall and unfortunately hit your head.'

He ran the tip of his startlingly pink tongue over his lips but remained silent. Zena stayed there beside him, instinctively aware that he was in need of a comforting presence. Below his bandages his nose was aristocratic with flared nostrils, and already a black stubble had grown on his chin and the sides of his face. As the silence lengthened she spoke to him softly, asking whether there was anything he wanted. She saw his lips tremble as he tried to form some words, and waited.

At last the words seemed wrenched from him. 'Am . . . am . . . oh God! I am a coward.'

Zena pulled the stool from under his bed, sat on it and took his hand in her own. 'Tell me, what is worrying you? I am here to help you, you know.'

'Are . . . are we alone?'

'Yes, you are in a side-ward and it is quite private.'

'To . . . to be shot in the head . . . that is very serious, is it not?' he asked hoarsely.

'Well it certainly can be, a lot depends on the circumstances and also on the treatment. I can tell you that you were very fortunate in that you were operated on by one of the finest neuro-surgeons in England—and that means in the world. They sent up to London especially for him and you couldn't have had better or speedier attention. He is a marvellous surgeon.'

'I am most grateful for that. But . . . my sight? I am

unable to see . . . If he saved my life for me to be blind, I would sooner have died.' His hands gripped hers so strongly that she almost cried out.

'Blind? Of course you are not blind. You can't see because your eyes are bandaged. I have seen the report on your condition and there is no mention of your optic nerve having been damaged. So really you are worrying unnecessarily, and that is not going to do you any good at all. Believe me, there is nothing for you to worry about, Mr Gharbally,' she said positively.

A slight sound or movement made her turn around. Mr Smythe, very large, very well-dressed, was standing just inside the door. How long he had been there she had no idea; it seemed to be a habit of his to creep up on people.

'There is somebody else here,' Mr Gharbally said accusingly, releasing her hand abruptly.

Zena patted his shoulder and rose to her feet. 'Yes. Mr Smythe, the surgeon who operated on you has just this minute arrived to see you.' She gave a brief nod to the surgeon. 'Good morning, sir.'

'Good morning, Sister. And good morning to you, Mr Gharbally. How are you today?'

When he had finished talking to his patient the surgeon followed Zena to her office. 'Would you care for some coffee, sir?' she asked.

'Thank you, I would.' He sat down, overlapping the small chair and stretching out his legs. 'When does your . . . Mr Moore, is it? . . . when does he get back from his leave?'

'He is actually returning from Elba tomorrow, but he is not officially on duty until the next day. However, he is very good, everybody feels comfortable when he is in the vicinity. He would be sure to come in if there was an emergency, as he lives only a few miles away,' she explained.

There was a tap on the door and Nurse Simmons, scarlet to the roots of her hair, placed a tray with a coffee-pot, milk jug, sugar-basin and two cups and saucers on the table. She gave a shy, side-long glance at Mr Smythe, who rewarded her with a heart-melting smile. Zena's mind boggled at the VIP treatment; never before had the coffee arrived in anything but a mug. What it was to have status! Was he subservient to anybody at all? Or was he the sturgeon in the hospital gold-fish pond?

'I see, he must be a very commendable man. I suppose if he had been somewhere in England he would have come hot-footing back to attend to Mr Gharbally?'

'Oh yes, without any doubt,' Zena said warmly.

'Then I will get away today. The patient seems to be coming along satisfactorily but with a head wound such as he had one can never be sure. There was a considerable degree of fractured bone, and some of the splinters were very small; it really needed micro-surgery, but there isn't the equipment here. A splinter can lie dormant for years and then for no apparent reason start to give trouble, but we hope that won't be so in this case.' He looked across at her with a provocative glint in his eyes. 'Tell me, Sister, on whose authority did you tell Mr Gharbally that he would not lose his sight?'

His words caught at her heart and she gave a gasp of dismay. She spoke indignantly. 'There is nothing on his chart to suggest that his optic nerve had been damaged, and I have always been able to rely on the information on the patient's chart.' Her voice shook. 'It hasn't been, has it?'

His grey eyes stared into hers as he said authoritatively, 'No, it hasn't, Sister. But there are other things. He might have a thrombosis of the central artery of the retina which could cause blindness, in which case you would have to break the news to him and at the same time reveal that your word is not to be relied on. A double blow, don't you agree?'

Zena felt a great urge to attack this smooth-talking unfeeling man. She clenched her fists under her desk. 'But I had to say something to comfort him, the poor man was so tensed up . . . so terrified . . . and that

wasn't doing him any good at all. He said he would
rather have died than become blind.'

'A normal reaction, you might say. What is one
supposed to do in those circumstances? Wait until he is
conscious and ask him to make the choice? By then it
would be too late if he opted for being blind. But this is
stupid talk. How long have you been a sister?'

'How long?' She looked at him with startled eyes.
'Why . . . s . . . six months . . . well, nearly.' Never had
it sounded so short a time.

There was a pause and she stared fixedly at his fine
grey socks and expensive leather shoes.

'You surprise me, you are reacting more like a first-
year nurse,' he said, a tinge of rebuke in his voice.

A fierce rush of injured pride brought the colour
flooding to her cheeks, making her eyes sparkle angrily.
'Sir?' she said in a clipped voice.

He spoke levelly and deliberately as if he was teaching
a rather backward student. 'Nobody can have told you
whether or not Mr Gharbally will lose his sight, for I
myself do not know. It is not the function of a nurse to
jump to conclusions. If the unfortunate patient is
blinded then your job is to do your best to help him to
come to terms with the affliction. If you become emo-
tionally involved you are not working in his best in-
terests; you must surely have learnt that. Be careful that
you do not forget it.' He pushed himself up from his
chair and made his way casually to the window.

'You . . . I know all that . . . I . . .' Zena choked over
the words in her rage.

He swung around and looked straight at her, his
warning eyes silencing her. She bit her lip hard, breaking
the skin. Then after a heart-jerking moment said in a
strangled voice, 'Thank you, sir.'

He smoothed the recalcitrant lock of hair from his
forehead with a well-manicured hand. 'Yes. Well, I will
be leaving now. If there is any deterioration in the
patient's condition, I want to know, whether your Mr
Moore has returned or not. Here is my Harley Street

number; if I am not there they will know where to contact me. And . . . many thanks for the coffee.' He walked to the door, then with his hand on the knob, turned and smiled. It was a smile of such sweetness, spreading from his eyes to his mouth, that his whole personality changed and she felt surrounded by warmth, and weightless, as if she were floating on a cloud in the sunshine. 'I must thank you for the splendid testimonial you gave me, Sister. I promise you I will try to live up to it. And to think they say that listeners never hear any good of themselves!' Before she could make any reply he had gone.

She covered her face with her hands and listened until the sound of his footsteps had died away, hearing them despite the clatter of bedpans and the rattle of trolleys. Not for years had anyone had this power to churn her feelings, to make her feel vulnerable and insecure. Nowadays it was she who stressed the rules, who criticised others and knew that merely by appearing in the ward or raising her eyebrows she kept the nurses and patients on their toes. Even the doctors asked and valued her opinion. So Edgwarebury Hospital might not be in the same class as his London hospitals, the doctors here might not have reached his dizzy heights, but a ward sister was surely someone to be reckoned with. How dared he speak to her as if she was a student. How dared he! Well, of course he dared, he could do and say what he liked. Coffee in a coffee-pot and on a tray, indeed! She pressed the bell furiously for the nurse to take it away, the silly little nurse who blushed to look at him. Thank goodness he had gone now and with any luck she might never see him again.

The door opened and her head jerked up afraid lest he had returned, but it was the round and cheerful face of Dr Owens that appeared around it.

'Ah, I hoped I'd catch you before you went to lunch.' He was a jolly young man but today his eyes looked strained and there were lines of fatigue on his face. 'My patient is on his way to the ward. He was in a nasty mess, his ulcer had perforated. I'd like him on half-hourly observations to be on the safe. Okay?'

'Right you are,' Zena said, making a note on her pad. 'That's Mr Cotton, isn't it?'

Dr Owens rubbed his forehead with his knuckles and nodded. 'I think he'll be all right. I hope so, but he left it pretty late. Apparently he had been having severe pain for years but had dosed himself with soda bic. instead of seeing his GP.'

Zena made an impatient gesture. 'That does annoy me. It is so stupid; anyone with a grain of sense should know that the sooner an illness is diagnosed and dealt with the better the chance of recovery.'

He thrust his hands in his coat pockets. 'That's true, of course. But who am I to speak? Doctors are worse than anybody at neglecting symptoms in themselves, and in their own families. My father was a doctor and he positively ignored any aches or pains we complained about. Mum used to say we would have to die to get him to take any notice.'

Zena laughed. 'Well, they say a cobbler's child is ill-shod and it's only natural a doctor wants to feel free of his work when he is at home. By the way, I wanted to have a word with you about Mrs Day. She is complaining of having quite a bit of pain.'

'Mrs Day? That's the gall-bladder, isn't it?'

Zena picked out a chart and handed it to him. 'Her temperature is fluctuating quite a lot.'

He studied it for a moment. 'Let's see, how long is it now? Oh it's quite early days; it wasn't a straightforward operation. It'll take time. We'll give her this.' He wrote on her chart and passed it back. 'That should ease the pain. And you'd better do three-hourly checks for the next twenty-four hours.' He raised his arms above his head and yawned hugely. 'I'll be glad to have the old man back; it'll be good to know he's around.'

Zena nodded. 'Yes, it never seems the same without him.' Then she asked casually, 'What did you think of Mr Smythe?'

Ben let out a sigh of admiration. 'What a man! What a surgeon! I've always considered Mr Moore to be the tops and of course he is, but watching this bloke was out of this world. His hands worked like magic.'

'All surgeons need skilful hands,' she said acidly.

He looked ruefully at his own. 'He made me feel as if my fingers were large pork sausages. Thanks heavens he was available; I could never have done it myself. The trouble is, he has given me the most awful feeling of inferiority. I feel I'm in the wrong job and should have been a butcher.'

'Nonsense, you will be just as good in time, it's only that he has had more experience. But what did you think of him as a person?' She pretended to be occupied with reading some notes.

There was silence for a moment and she looked up questioningly to see him smiling down at her. 'Et tu, Sister?'

'Et tu, what?'

'Don't tell me you're another one!'

'I wish you wouldn't talk in riddles; you make me feel like half of a music-hall turn. All right then. Another one of what?'

His smile widened to a grin. 'Another one who has fallen for him hook, line and sinker.'

'What on earth do you mean?' She wrinkled her nose at him.

'Every female who came within a mile of him was smitten by his olde worlde charm, from old Mrs Reynolds, pushing eight, to young Nurse Simmons who they say will never be the same again and stands about staring into space. Can you be yet another, Sister dear?' His brown eyes, cheeky as a monkey's, teased her.

She sprang up from her chair, knocking it so much that it toppled over. 'Olde worlde charm! Him! Honestly, I've never heard such rubbish. I merely asked how you got on with him, because far from being "smitten" by him, which is a word I can't stand anyway, I disliked him intensely. I thought he was a conceited, self-opinionated man and too pleased with himself by half. I'm jolly glad he is going back where he came from and I hope we never have to ask for his help again!' Zena exploded.

Ben ran to the door, cowering in mock alarm. Then, when he had opened it and gone outside, he put his head around it and said softly: 'Methinks the lady doth protest too much!'

'Oh, you!' Zena threw a book in his direction. He hastily closed the door and to her intense irritation she heard him chuckling as he went down the corridor.

CHAPTER THREE

THE following week slid by. There were the usual admittances and discharges forming an ever recurring pattern of nervous strangers arriving, the hospital speedily becoming as familiar to them as their home. Then came the fond farewells to their bed-mates who had so soon become friends, because of the fellow-feeling created by the unique circumstances.

When it was suggested that Mrs Bottome was well enough to return home she developed respiratory trouble, reminding Zena that there was frequently some underlying medical reason for a patient's difficult behaviour. Mrs Day, on the other hand, was making an excellent recovery and had stopped complaining of pain. At the end of the week she would be moving on to a convalescent home.

Mr Moore had returned from his holiday in Elba enviously sun-tanned. It had been decided that Mr Gharbally's bandages could be removed today, and Zena found herself praying silently and fervently that all would be well. Each day she had spent an increasingly long time by his bedside in response to his mute appeal for reassurance. With others of the staff he was abrupt and withdrawn as if he resented their necessary attentions, so that when she could arrange it, Zena tended him herself. He told her that his home was in Kuwait but he had been to both public school and university in England where he had obtained a degree in engineering. They spoke often of the mysteries of life and death, but underlying these discussions was his persistent dread, the fear that he might be blind. Remembering the autocratic Mr Smythe's warning she was careful not to build his hopes too high, but to be scrupulously honest. Together they considered the many difficulties that a blind person would face and worked out ways of surmounting them, so that it became almost a game, albeit a macabre one.

One day when their conversation had ended on a happy note he said: 'You are a most wonderful person. With someone like you beside me I believe I could face anything at all. You give me faith in myself and courage I never imagined I could have.'

Zena felt a warm glow of pleasure. It was for this sort of reaction that she had wanted to enter the nursing profession. 'I'm glad about that, Mr Gharbally, it always pleases us as nurses to know that we have been able to help a patient. That is what nursing is about.'

He fumbled for her hand and held it between both of his. 'I do not get the same feeling with the other nurses, I believe they do not care. They do their job but . . . maybe it is because they are young, too young to appreciate my fears. As an older woman you are someone I have supreme confidence in. You are almost like another father.'

Zena withdrew her hand. 'Father? Don't you mean mother?'

'Of course it is different in England; I forgot. In my country our father is the head of our household, we look to him for help and guidance in everything. You have not married, Sister?'

She paused for a moment. 'No. I have always been too busy working to think of getting married.'

He said thoughtfully, 'Ah, then I understand. You give all your love and attention to your patients, that is plain.'

She left him then, and brooded over what he had said. She knew he had not got it right. She did her best for her patients, and enjoyed her work, but she would not like to spend her whole life in nursing. Sometimes the rigidity of the rules, the endless demands of the patients, to say nothing of her colleagues, irritated her unbearably. One day she wanted to be free of them all, to have a man of her own, and children, and it was to them that she would give all her love and attention. The feelings she would have for them would be lasting and quite different from those she had for her patients, because when they had left the hospital it was not long before she forgot them completely, and they her, as she well knew. But there is an exception to every rule and she was confident that whatever the outcome, whether Sami Gharbally would be able to see or not when his bandages were removed, she would never forget him. She was deeply involved with him in his fears and his hopes, and they had made an imprint on her heart and in her mind which could never be entirely eradicated.

Later on Dr Owens joined her in her office and Nurse Simmons brought them two cups of coffee and placed them on her desk. After she had gone Zena said rebelliously, 'When Mr Smythe had coffee here with me it was brought in on a tray, with coffee-pot, milk-jug and all. How's that for preferential treatment?'

Ben grinned in his engaging way. 'That's life, that's what he slogged his guts out for, to get coffee in a coffee-pot in Edgewarebury Hospital. That's what it's all about, luv.'

'At what point in one's career, I wonder, does one graduate from a cup to a pot?' Zena eyed him thoughtfully.

Ben ran his capable fingers through his hair. 'You have got it in for that poor chap, haven't you? At what point did we graduate from a plastic mug to a china cup? Do you remember? Do you even care? Because I don't. All I know is that if I had a fraction of the skill Smythe has I would expect the coffee-pot to be made of solid silver at least. And lined with gold.'

'Oh well.' Zena raised a disdainful shoulder. 'Of course you saw him at work and I didn't have that . . .' She hesitated.

'Privilege is the word you are looking for, luv,' Ben said earnestly.

'Is it?'

There was a pause as Ben thoughtfully surveyed her

over his cup. Then he said, changing the subject, 'Mr Moore says Mr Gharbally's bandages can come off today. I am expecting him to come along this morning.'

'Then I hope your wonder-boy lives up to your high opinion of him and has made a thumping success of the op.' And under her breath she repeated fervently, 'I do hope so!'

Ben replaced his cup on the saucer and fiddled with the spoon. 'He did everything possible that any surgeon could do. If this chap's sight is impaired it is the gunman you must blame, not Smythe.'

'Oh, yes, I know that,' Zena said hastily, her voice apologetic. 'I know I sound bitchy but I am desperately worried about Mr Gharbally. You must put it down to that.'

Ben stood up and leaned on the back of his chair. 'There have been other cases. I've never known you to be so concerned before.'

'Oh Ben,' she protested. 'I'm always concerned; I always care.'

He turned on her a long, searching look. 'In my opinion you have become too involved with this patient, and it doesn't do, you know.'

She gave an exasperated sigh. 'Of course I haven't!' Then in a softer voice she added, 'But he somehow seems exceptionally vulnerable. I feel I would do anything to stop him being hurt.'

He raised his eyebrows. 'But you can't, of course. The most you can do is help him come to terms with whatever he has to face. He is a man.'

'But to be blind! You make it sound so easy when you say I should help him come to terms with it. But can you imagine what it would be like? To be able to see normally one moment and then . . . in a split second . . . see nothing for the rest of your life?'

'Pretty horrible,' Ben admitted. 'But unfortunately not unique.' He glanced at his watch. 'I must be away. Thanks for the coffee . . .' He winked and gave a sly smile. 'Even in a cup it tasted OK to me. And try not to worry; it may never happen.' He sketched a salute and loped away.

Zena still sat there, her chin resting on her hands, her eyes blank as she mulled over Sami Gharbally's prospects. She longed yet dreaded to hear the outcome of the operation. How he must be suffering, not just with the pain which had been considerable, but mentally, as he wondered every minute of every hour of every day what the result would be. Zena squeezed her eyes tight. It would be dark like that all the time; it did not bear thinking about, never to see a flower or a tree, a sunrise or a sunset, never to see a baby smile. To be cut off from reading and unable to work until he had learned anew. 'Oh God,' she prayed, 'Please, please don't let it be like that.' Suddenly she thought—if he is able to see, what is he going to think of his surroundings? She sprang from her chair and sped along the corridor to his room, acknowledging people as they passed but not really aware of them.

Sami Gharbally lay quite still in the bare antiseptic room, his chin and the area around his mouth shadowed dark with bristles, his badly pressed hospital issue pyjamas done up on the wrong buttons. Something inside Zena began to ache at the sight.

'Hello, Mr Gharbally,' she said cheerfully.

'Sister.' His hands reached out and she took them in hers. 'Mr Moore will be along shortly to take off your bandages. You will feel much better without them; they are probably the cause of some of your headaches.'

'Sister . . . I . . . I feel terrible,' he whispered.

She squeezed his hands. 'Of course. But it won't be long now.'

He ran his tongue across his lips. 'I . . . I am such a coward. I am afraid for when they come off. How you must despise me, for I despise myself.'

She wanted desperately to hold him in her arms and comfort him, but she said briskly, 'Now you mustn't talk such nonsense. Far from despising you I admire you very

much. You have been distressed, but that is not to be
wondered at, and on top of everything else you are in a
strange country.' She released his hands. 'You haven't
had a shave today. How is that?'

'It is not the nurse's fault, I wouldn't let her do it.'

'I see. Well, you try stopping me!'

When she had shaved him so that his skin was velvety
smooth to touch she tidied his bed and arranged the
window curtains neatly. Then, unashamedly, she went
into the main ward and came back with some vases of
particularly nice flowers and put them on the sill. She
went through the pile of pyjamas until she found a brand
new pair for him to change into.

'There you are, thoroughly spoilt, Mr Gharbally. Is
there anything else you want?' She found herself thinking of the sort of reply she would get if she asked such an
unwise question of any man in the main ward, but Sami
said, 'No thank you, Sister, you are so very good to me.'

'It's all part of the service,' she told him briskly. 'Mr
Moore may be a little later than we thought, because he
has an emergency to attend to.'

'Another emergency! That is a way of life to doctors
and nurses, isn't it? I, who am so important to myself am
just one of many cases; I have no identity. I have heard
the nurses refer to me as "the one in the side ward" and
that is all I am. If I were to die in here nobody would ever
remember my name.'

She laughed indulgently. 'You silly boy, you want me
to say that isn't true, don't you? Well I'm not going to. If
you don't know better than that by now it's too bad. As
for dying in here, well, you aren't going to, or anywhere
else, not for the foreseeable future, and if you don't stop
feeling so sorry for yourself I shall lose patience with
you.'

'Don't be cross with me, Sister,' he pleaded.

'Oh yes, I will be unless you cheer up. Now I must go;
all this talk is just a ploy to keep me here.'

When she had reached the door he said urgently, 'You
will be here when my bandages come off, won't you?'

Zena thought of the work piling up in her office and knew that normally it would be Sue who would be in attendance with Mr Moore. But if it was humanly possible she would be here in case he needed her as she knew he would if things turned out badly for him. 'I'll come along if I can,' she replied non-committally.

She heard her phone ringing before she reached her office and hurried to answer it. A young man with an inflamed appendix was being sent up from Casualty. He was suffering severe pain and rigidity of the abdomen and was clearly in need of immediate surgery. As Zena was arranging with a nurse that a bed should be prepared for him, Mr Moore arrived. Despite his newly acquired sun-tan he looked tired and very annoyed. 'I've just wasted valuable time on a stupid girl who took an overdose. I've got more important people to attend to, patients who are ill through no fault of their own. She knew perfectly well she would be found in time, as most of them do. No sooner had she swallowed the wretched things than she called for help.'

'She must have been dreadfully unhappy, though,' Zena said slowly.

He snorted. 'So are thousands of people. Say we all took an overdose when we felt a bit down? Anyhow, it's over to you. She's being sent up here for a day or so.'

'Up here? She's not a surgical case, is she?'

'No she isn't, but there are no beds spare anywhere else.'

'That leaves me with no spares. Say we get an emergency?'

'In that case we will have to off-load someone to the cottage hospital. But we'll keep our fingers crossed. Maybe someone can be discharged in the next few days.'

'Are you going to see Mr Gharbally now?' Zena asked anxiously.

'Not yet. Mr Smythe is coming down for the grand re-opening. Apparently he wants to be in at the death.'

The words were spoken casually in Mr Moore's usual flippant style, which in reality covered a great caring, but today the words were like a whiplash to Zena and she could make no reply.

'In the meantime I will take a look at the appendix chappie.'

Soon after Mr Moore had gone, a porter trundling a trolley stopped at her door and handed her some papers. She thanked him and glanced briefly at the young girl who lay there.

'Go straight through, Mick. Nurse is preparing a bed. I think she is ready for you.'

When he had wheeled the empty trolley away Zena went to speak to the new patient. She was only in her teens and although Zena understood and to a certain extent shared Mr Moore's disgust at attempted suicides, she nevertheless had a feeling of pity and dismay that a person could be so desperately unhappy. She drew the screens around the bed and studied the face on the pillow. The eyes were heavily drugged but open. She had a large wide vulnerable mouth and fair hair that hung in dull strands over her shoulders.

'I'm sorry, I'm sorry,' she murmured over and over again.

'Yes, well, it's all over now. You'll go to sleep and when you wake up everything will be much brighter, you'll see,' Zena said briskly.

'I didn't want to die . . . I just took them because I didn't want to go on living,' she muttered.

'That sounds pretty mixed up to me, but don't you worry about it, dear.'

'They were all so beastly to me, all of them,' she whimpered.

Zena, who had been pulling back the curtains came back to her. 'Who? The girls at school? The girls you work with? Your parents?'

'No.' She gave a little sob. 'The nurses and doctors here, they were all horrible.'

'You mustn't worry about that, dear, they were cross because you caused a lot of unnecessary work, but mostly because they don't like the idea of people trying to kill themselves when they spend their time trying to keep them alive. Still, never mind, love, it's over now. When you have had a nice sleep you'll feel a different person.'

'Will you be here?' The girl raised her eyes appealingly, and immediately Zena thought of Sami and her promise to him. 'I'll be on the ward,' she said, patting her shoulder.

She streaked along the corridor to Sami's room. Yes, they were all there. Sue was unwinding the bandages, revealing more and more of the thick black hair. Mr Moore in his neat dark suit, stood at the foot of the bed and beside him was Mr Symthe. He was standing nonchalantly, a hand in his trouser pocket, an oblong gold watch showing beneath his cuff. Zena caught her breath as she looked at him but neither he nor Mr Moore turned to see who had entered; they were intent on watching Sue. As the last of the bandages came away there was a moment of silence as if the world had stood still. Then Mr Symthe's cool authoritative voice said smoothly, 'Right, Mr Gharbally, you can open your eyes now.'

The long black lashes fluttered against the ivory cheeks, lifted fractionally, then fell again.

'Try again, please. Tell me what you can see.'

Sami's eyelids were slowly raised until they revealed eyes that were almost black. He blinked several times, brushed the back of his hand across his face, then opened his eyes wide. 'I can see! I can see! Thanks be to God!' he cried exultantly.

As congratulations were bandied to and fro Zena felt a great tide of relief. 'I am delighted, Mr Gharbally; this is splendid news,' she beamed.

His face became a mask of bewilderment as he stared at her. 'You . . . you are Sister Foster? But you can't be . . . you are so young. I . . . I thought . . .'

Mr Smythe interrupted whatever it was he had been going to say by moving forward and holding a finger up in front of him. 'I want you to follow my finger with your eyes, please. Don't move your head.'

He held up more fingers. 'How many fingers can you see? And now?'

When he had completed his tests he laid his hand briefly on Sami's shoulder. 'That's splendid, Mr Gharbally, everything seems to be in working order. Have you any pain? Any headaches?'

'I sometimes have headaches, Doctor, but they are nothing. I can bear them so long as I have my sight.'

Mr Smythe studied his face for a moment, then gave a nod of satisfaction. 'It could have been worrying about the outcome that caused your headaches. Worry can do a great deal of harm. When you are up and about they will probably disappear. Well now, I don't see any need to keep you in hospital much longer. Mr Moore and Sister will have a little chat about it and let you know when you can go home.'

Sami turned his large dark eyes on him. 'I must thank you most sincerely for what you have done for me. Everyone is telling me what a wonderful surgeon you are and how fortunate I was that you operated on me. I shall always be indebted to you.'

Mr Smythe turned aside with a look of embarrassment on his face. 'Not at all, Mr Gharbally, it is my job. Anyhow, it's nice to have a satisfied customer.'

As he was leaving the room with Mr Moore, his cool grey eyes rested for a moment on Zena. She stared back at him but was the first to turn away. When Sue had returned to the ward and she was alone with Sami, she said: 'Well, Mr Gharbally, you must be feeling happier now. You're glad it's all over?'

Without his bandages she saw that he was a handsome man. Beneath well-defined eyebrows his eyes were as gentle and kind as his mouth. As they looked at her now they kindled with warmth. 'Sister Foster, I can hardly believe it is you. How terrible to think that if I had been blind I should never have seen you, never have had that privilege.' His open admiration made her turn aside shyly. 'Would that have mattered so much? People are what they are regardless of their appearance. In a way I think it is possible to assess people better when you cannot see them. You have nothing to prejudice your judgment.'

He replied softly, 'I knew you to be kind and understanding and patient and helpful, everything any woman could be, but I thought you were a much older woman—maybe homely in appearance—with threads of silver in your hair. If I had known you were so young I would not have allowed you to do the things you did for me. I should not have spoken to you of my fears. I would not have let you see me weep. And now I am deeply ashamed.' His lashes cast long shadows on his cheeks and the corners of his mouth tightened.

'Then I am very glad that you couldn't see me,' Zena said firmly. 'You needed help, you needed to talk to someone, and as for tears . . . it always makes me angry when men think it is weak to cry, that it is something only women can do. Tears are meant to be shed, they are a great relief in times of stress and as natural as laughter. You don't feel ashamed when you smile. Never underestimate the value of tears, and never be ashamed of them, Mr Gharbally.'

He plucked at the counterpane. 'To weep for other people's suffering, for the injustices of the world is permissible, I agree. But to weep for oneself . . . surely that is self-pity which you told me was bad?'

Zena nodded. 'That is true, of course. If you kept on being miserable about something that had happened to yourself, some loss you had sustained, whether it was a loved one or a home or your sight, that would be self-pity, and very wrong because sooner or later you have to be brave and come to terms with it. But initially it is only human nature to grieve and I, for one, would cry my eyes out.'

'Sister,' he said suddenly. 'When will I be leaving?'

Zena jerked as if someone had jabbed a needle in her. This was the pattern of a nurse's life, the facet of it which she found so difficult to come to terms with. You could become so close to a patient, get very fond of them so that their worries were your problems and feel that they really liked you in return. Then suddenly you realised that they were eager to leave, to return to their normal life and that after all you meant nothing to them. It happened all the time and was a healthy sign for it meant the patient had recovered. Over the years you became reconciled, knowing it was proper and inevitable. But with Mr Gharbally there had seemed a deeper bond between them, one which would not be easily broken. She had thought he would be reluctant to leave, maybe a little sad, but after all she was mistaken. She gave a professional smile.

'Dear me, you are in a hurry to go, aren't you? Anyone would think we hadn't made you comfortable. All right, you can go home tomorrow—no, the day after. I would like you to walk around a bit first, to find your feet. Is there somebody at home to cook for you?' Yet as she asked the question she remembered he had had no visitors.

'I am in England on business and am staying at a hotel so that will be no problem. But I shall miss being here. When I ring my bell it will not be you who will answer it,' he said sadly.

'Come now, Mr Gharbally, you know perfectly well that I don't come running to your call,' she scoffed.

'You would come if I asked for you,' he said, his lashes half-covering his eyes.

'Only when you were ill. Now that you are better I doubt if I would come near you.'

He turned his face to his pillow. 'Then I might as well leave. There is nothing to keep me here.'

Zena walked determinedly to the door. 'Quite clearly you are better! Your clothes are hanging in the cupboard and the bathroom is just along the corridor. Have a bath, get dressed, then walk up and down the corridor or in the men's ward . . . the *men's* ward, mind!' she ended with a smile.

He looked at her with a disconsolate expression on his face. 'Can I sit in your office?'

'No, you can't,' she said firmly. 'I am afraid there isn't anywhere much that you can go. Once a patient is mobile he is better off at home . . . or in your case, your hotel. I must go now. Lie on your bed if you feel like it.'

She walked briskly away, moving quickly as if to get away from the ache in her heart. She was guiltily aware that despite all warnings and all her own denials, she had committed the stupid and unforgivable sin of falling in love with a patient.

CHAPTER FOUR

It being Sunday, there were no operations or doctor's rounds. Visitors, however, arrived in their hordes bearing fruit which in many cases rotted in the dishes on the bedside lockers, and flowers for which enough vases could not be found so that previous offerings, still almost in their prime, had to be thrown away in the already overflowing bins. Children who were once banned from the wards were now allowed in, and boredom made them restless, noisy and tearful.

Zena hoped that Sue or somebody would drop into her office for a chat, to dispel the depression which had enveloped her. It felt like the mist she remembered as a child, which came off the Cornish sea, blotting out the cliffs and the countryside and settling in beads of moisture on hair and clothes; accentuated by a mournful fog-horn.

It was three days since Sami Gharbally had been discharged. He had come to her office to say goodbye, wearing a well-cut suit and cream silk shirt and looking so different from the bandaged man in crumpled hospital-issue pyjamas that she scarcely recognised him. Dr Owens was with her at the time. Sami shook hands with them both, gave a small, almost imperceptible, bow, thanked them profusely for their care and kindness and walked away down the corridor to wait for the lift. When it arrived he did not even look back. Zena knew, because she was watching.

'There he goes, as good as new,' Ben Owens said casually.

And that was it. Now that he had been satisfactorily dealt with he had left. He had not given them the name of his hotel for there was no need. So now he had disappeared without trace. All the concern and care and fervent prayers for his recovery leading up to the climax when he had his bandages removed and the result of his operation had been assured, had suddenly come to an end and were not needed any more. The trouble, Zena decided, was that there had been no period of convalescence, when normally you gradually withdrew your support and concern for the patient. Instead, it had been a case of bandages off, all's well, and now you can leave. It had been too quick, it was as if a limb had been amputated and a part of you was missing.

She had scarcely seen Sami that last day and had no opportunity to speak with him again. The patient who had attempted suicide had needed her sympathy and attention, and Zena had no intention of stinting either. Another patient who had been making splendid progress had a sudden embolism and died and there were his relatives to be told, explanations to be made and sympathy given. It all took time. She pushed some papers and walked over to the window. Down below was the unloading bay where on weekdays laden lorries arrived and there was the business of men unloading them and wheeling the supplies to the various store-houses. Today it was empty and everywhere was locked up. There was no trickle of patients walking up the ramp to the Chest clinic and the balconies were empty of convalescents. Only the car park was full, hundreds of gleaming metal boxes standing tightly boot to bonnet with not a vacant space as drivers cruising slowly around the blocks discovered.

Zena sighed. She was tired of this view from the window, tired of the patients' complaints, tired of the food which tasted the same whatever they called it and most of all tired of expending her emotions on other people. For as far back as she could remember she had been studying for examinations, working when other people were not. Anti-social hours it was called and the union was trying to get them more money for that. But it was not the money that mattered, it was the loneliness when you were off duty. In the nature of things Sue was on duty when she was off and Sue was her only intimate friend. And now she was twenty-six. Would she spend the next thirty-four years here in this same hospital? Doing the same work? Seeing the same things?

The door opened and in bustled Sue. 'Tea's up,' she said cheerfully. 'Shall I have mine in here with you? With any luck I've got a few minutes.'

Zena pulled out another chair. 'Oh yes, lovely! I was hoping you would drop in.'

An ancillary worker popped her head around the door. 'Tea for two? Sugar?'

Sue took them from her and also a plate of biscuits. 'Good. Bourbons and wafers; we're being spoilt. I do like a nice sweet biscuit, don't you?'

'No,' Zena said morosely.

Sue chuckled. 'All right, I'll eat the lot. So what's wrong with biscuits all of a sudden?'

'I'd like chocolate éclairs and meringues for a change,' Zena said childishly.

'And who wouldn't? But just think how the NHS bill would soar!' Sue frowned in mock rebuke. 'As ward sister you should think of such things. On consideration I think I would be better at the job than you are.' She bit into a biscuit and a deluge of crumbs sprayed down over her plumped-out apron.

'I believe you would,' Zena admitted. 'You're always bright and breezy. I don't think anything ever gets you down.'

Sue gave a quick smile. 'Oh I have my moments the same as everyone else. What's biting you?'

'Nothing really. Just a Sunday feeling and seeing myself doing the same things, sitting at the same desk until I'm sixty.'

'Good heavens girl, what a way to think! Live one day at a time, you never know what's going to turn up,' Sue said briskly.

The telephone rang and Zena glared at it. 'Here we go again,' she said snatching up the receiver. Suddenly a smile lit up her face bringing pink to her cheeks. 'Mr

Gharbally! What a surprise. Is everything all right?' Her eyes became a deeper blue as she listened. 'Well, yes,' he said in reply. 'That would be lovely. Wednesday, three o'clock at Knightsbridge station. I shall look forward to that.'

'So what did I tell you?' Sue said triumphantly as Zena replaced the receiver.

'Oh you know everything, don't you?' Zena said, dimpling. 'But you are quite right. Life is wonderful; you never know what is waiting round the corner.'

'True,' Sue said cheerfully. 'But I know perfectly well what is waiting for me. Getting rid of the visitors, tidying the ward and doing the medicine round. We haven't all got good-looking oil-sheikhs eager to wine and dine us.'

'Silly,' Zena protested, laughing. 'Mr Gharbally is an engineer not an oil-sheikh and we are meeting for a cup of tea. But all the same it is really super to have a date on my day off.'

What she meant was that it was wonderful that she had not been forgotten; to see Sami Gharbally again, to continue their conversations and to share the happiness he would now be feeling.

Wednesday found Zena with various suits and dresses tossed on to her bed as she decided what she should wear. It had been a fairly warm morning which gave promise of a warmer afternoon. But if . . . just supposing they spent the evening in town, she would need something suitable for the homeward journey. She chose a blue suit and brushed her hair into a knot in the nape of her neck. Her complexion needed only a minimum of make-up, a smear of blue around her eyes and a touch of coral on her lips. She studied herself in the mirror trying to see herself through Sami's eyes. She put on pearl stud earrings to lessen the severity of her appearance but they did nothing to make her look more feminine. She tried knotting a chiffon scarf at her neck but it was too fussy. She was about to change into a dress but a quick glance at the clock told her she must hurry.

As a last resort she took the pins from her hair and brushed it so that it fell to her shoulders in a deep wave and in doing so shed a half-dozen years from her age.

She ran down the stairs and out of the hostel and along the path which led to the hospital gates. With a clanking sound a car moved slowly over the barriers and she stood by the porter's lodge until it was through. She glanced casually at the driver and her pulses leapt as her eyes met the cool grey gaze of Mr Smythe. She caught her breath sharply, her mouth felt too tight to stretch into a smile. His eyes widened slightly and rested on her for a moment longer than they need have done. Then he gave a brief nod of recognition, his lips formed the word 'sister' and the car slid forward, increasing its speed. And suddenly the pleasurable anticipation of seeing Sami fractionally lessened. She wondered who the surgeon was visiting today, then she remembered that he was one of the consultants who visited all the group hospitals at times although she had not seen him before he operated on Sami.

Now that she was on her way to meet Sami, Zena felt a tension, an inhibition. Talking to a patient who could not see her and speaking words of comfort was vastly different from taking part in a social conversation. What would they talk about?

She arrived five minutes early at her destination. There was no sign of Sami so she wandered along the road and glanced idly in shop windows until it was time to return to the station entrance. She wondered how long she should wait, she must give him a certain amount of leeway for a dozen things could delay him. Yet every minute seemed an hour. She looked carefully at the well-dressed people as they passed by, but none of them was the man she was to meet. She glanced at her watch. Six minutes past three. She had been waiting no time at all, it was her nursing training that made her a stickler for punctuality. Then suddenly she saw him standing beside a wall, studying her. With a feeling of relief she went across to him and he took a few steps towards her.

'Hello, Mr Gharbally, didn't you recognise me?'

He held out his hand. 'Not at first, but eventually I did. I have been watching you for some time.'

She felt a stab of embarrassed annoyance. 'Why were you doing that? Were you wondering how long I would wait?' She could read nothing in his opaque eyes.

'How long would you have waited?' he hedged.

She gave a brief laugh. 'Not much longer. I thought you might have been held up in the traffic. Had I known you were already here and merely watching my discomfiture I should not have waited at all.'

He laid his hand on her arm. 'Please do not say that. Shall we have some tea now? Then we can talk properly.'

They agreed on her favourite restaurant and were able to sit at her usual corner table. The waitress who took their order was one whom Zena frequently saw there and she looked from one to the other of them curiously.

'Do you realise,' Sami said when she had gone, 'I only saw you twice and you looked vastly different from today? I think it was clever of me to recognise you.'

'Of course! I had quite forgotten, because I was seeing you all the time. Not all of your face of course, but from the nose down.'

His eyes rested on her hair. 'I knew your hair was very fair but I only saw it pinned tightly under your cap. I had no idea it was so beautiful, Zena. May I call you that? And will you call me Sami?'

She laughed, delighted at his admiration. 'How does it feel to be up and about again? You haven't had any trouble, Sami?'

He lowered his silky lashes. 'Alas, I am unable to sleep.'

Zena's professional mind turned to his injuries seeking some reason for his insomnia. 'Do you have any pain? Or discomfort?'

He shook his head.

'Are you normally a good sleeper?'

'Always.'

Zena frowned thoughtfully. 'You have no idea what is causing it?'

He glanced at her through his lashes as he took the tea she passed him. 'Yes, I know why I cannot sleep, it is because of you. I keep wanting to hear your voice, to know that you are near me. Is that very wrong of me?'

Zena liked the words that were being said but she knew they were a hangover from a nurse-patient relationship and not to be taken seriously.

'I'll have to make a tape recording of myself saying "Goodnight Sami, sleep well. Have you everything you want?" Then you can play it over a few times. Only a few, I promise you, for you will soon forget the hospital, the accident and me. We will be a part of a nightmare,' she laughed.

His eyes probed hers. 'Is that what you truly think? Or what you want to believe?'

'Both, Sami.' Then, eager to change the subject, she asked if he had returned to work.

'I am not working here in the way you mean. I have had appointments with several people and have just a few more to make before I return home.'

Zena knew she should have felt no reaction to that but she experienced a feeling of dismay. 'Do you live in Kuwait permanently, then?' she asked sadly.

He nodded. 'Yes, it is my home. I have spent several years in England but now my father wishes me to settle down in Kuwait.'

'You seem very fond of your father. Are you the only son?'

A smile spread over his face. 'The only son? No, my mother is a good wife, she has given birth to twelve children and seven of them are sons.'

'That is a large family by today's standards,' Zena said, picturing another eleven like Sami, all incredibly handsome. 'It must be lovely to have so many brothers and sisters.'

Sami looked pleased. 'We are good family people; it is very different from in this country. And we are very close. My father, too, is still young enough to have many more children.'

'Many more? Heavens, your country will become over-populated at that rate!'

He shook his head. 'Oh no, there are very few of us really, half of our population is made up of other nationalities, people who are employed in the oil-fields and in many of our public and private enterprises.' He counted off on his fingers. 'There are Iraqis, Egyptians, Syrians, Palestinians, Lebanese, Indians, Pakistanis, Americans and Europeans. We need to increase our Kuwaiti population or we will lose our identity, we are all worried about this.' He frowned as he contemplated the prospect. Then, remembering her presence, he asked Zena if she would like some pastries.

'Thank you, I would,' she said choosing a slice of strawberry gateau. 'I will get fat if I am not careful. I shall have to starve myself for a week to counteract this. Still, that won't be difficult with hospital food.'

His eyes wandered over her caressingly. 'You are beautiful as you are, but I should prefer that you were plumper so eat as many cakes as you can,' he said.

'That's easy talk, but you won't be here to see my corpulence. When are you going home?'

'At the end of the week if possible.'

'So soon! Will you be glad?'

He looked uncertain. 'Yes I will be happy to see my family but sorry that I will be so far from you, Zena.'

'I will be sorry too. But perhaps you will come back and visit us one day? For a holiday?'

'That is quite possible. Two of my brothers are coming here to finish their education. Maybe I will come over to see that they are behaving themselves.'

'Spoil-sport,' Zena laughed. 'What about your sisters? Will they come here?'

He drew his dark brows together. 'My sisters? Oh no, three of them are married and another will be getting married soon.'

Zena looked at him with surprise. 'Funny, I thought of you as being the eldest. I don't know why.'

'I am the eldest, I am thirty-four. Girls marry much younger, of course.'

Zena said, 'I seem to remember reading somewhere that in your country their marriages are arranged. Is that so?'

His voice hardened. 'Many of the young women nowadays insist on having more freedom than they had, but generally speaking they like their husbands to be chosen for them. It is customary for first cousins to marry for in that way the wealth and property stays in the family. It is a happy arrangement.'

Zena gave him a sideways smile. 'So have you a cousin lined up for yourself?'

He glanced ostentatiously at his watch but made no reply. After a while he said casually, 'I have two tickets for a theatre tonight if you would care to see the show. I forget what it is called.' He felt in his pocket for the tickets and passed them to her. 'Do you know what it is?'

Zena looked at them delightedly. 'No, I don't. I haven't been to the theatre for years so I shall love to see it whatever it is.'

Her pleasure in the forthcoming treat was slightly marred however by his snub in not replying to her question. Yet maybe it was something that would not have been asked in his country, perhaps she had been impolite. When they had finished tea they walked through the store for she was anxious to show him the luxurious merchandise.

'Have you ever seen anything so beautiful?' she asked when they were in the china department.

'No,' he replied, a mocking glint in his eyes. 'I am used to living in a mud hut and eating off the floor.'

She swung around in surprise. 'Are you really? I didn't . . .'

He gave a shout of laughter, showing his very white teeth. 'Zena, I wish you could see my country, it is, I think, about the wealthiest in the world. We have splendid shops and schools and hospitals and nice homes and furniture. You would like it very much.'

'You must think I am very ignorant but until I met you I didn't even know where Kuwait was!' she admitted apologetically.

'And you do now?'

'Oh yes, I know exactly where it is.'

'So you looked it up on the atlas?'

'Yes, that's right.'

He scanned her face. 'Because you wanted to know where my home was?'

Zena shrugged. 'I wanted to know where Kuwait was.'

'Because it was my home?' he persisted.

'If you like.'

'I do like,' he said softly. 'For that I shall buy you a little gift, some perfume, I think. In my country young ladies use many perfumes; it is not so over here.'

'I suppose you associate me with antiseptics,' Zena said ruefully.

He looked at her in surprise. 'Of course. It is your work and is right for you then. But tonight you will wear something more exotic.'

For Zena, unused as she was to luxuries, tonight was an occasion she would remember for a long time. The little gift of perfume proved to be a large flask of the most expensive on sale. The play was the latest musical in town, the seats the best, and Sami was beside her, courteous, affectionate and handsome. When at last the curtain came down she gave a sigh which was a mixture of regret and satisfaction.

'That was absolutely lovely, Sami. Thank you so much,' she said.

She refused his offer of supper knowing that it would make her late in getting back to the hospital, and said she would like to make her way to the station.

'Indeed no,' Sami replied firmly. 'We will take a taxi to the hospital and then it can take me to my hotel.'

In the taxi it was like being in a small world of their

own. Outside was a stream of traffic with its everlasting
dazzle of headlamps. Everywhere seemed busier, more
exciting than during the daytime. The back of their
driver was a blur through the glass and in their little
world was the heady scent of her perfume and the two of
them alone together. Sami's arm crept around her and
drew her against his warm body, pressed her head on his
shoulder.

'You are so beautiful, Zena,' he murmured, his lips
brushing her cheek. 'Every day and every night you are
in my mind and in my heart.' He caressed her cheek and
ran his fingers through her hair. 'It is like finest silk. And
your skin is so smooth and cool. My darling . . .' His
mouth covered hers, moving over it gently, lovingly. 'It
is so good to hold you close, to feel your body next to
mine. Until today I thought it might be that I loved you
as a child seeking comfort, but now I know it is as a man
wanting you as a woman.'

She slid her arms around his neck and saw in the lights
of passing cars the glitter of his eyes that sparkled like
jet, those eyes which both of them had feared might be
sightless. She stretched up and kissed them, first the one
and then the other in love and in thankfulness. He
covered her face with hard, passionate kisses that set her
heart thudding in her throat so that her breath could only
come in gasps. Suddenly the dividing window was
pushed back and the driver's Cockney voice interrupted
them, making her feel as if he had thrown a glass of cold
water over her.

'Here we are, sir, Edgwarebury Hospital. Where do
you want dropping off?'

Zena struggled to a sitting position and peered out of
the window. 'Here will do splendidly,' she said. Turning
to Sami she realised that the spell which had enveloped
them was completely shattered. She spoke politely like a
well-mannered child after a party. 'Goodbye and thank
you for giving me such a lovely time.'

Sami climbed out of the cab and held the door open
for her. 'It was my pleasure,' he replied formally.

They shook hands briefly, then he got back into the taxi and it drove away. Zena felt thwarted, cheated and empty. Once again at the height of their togetherness, when she felt that she and Sami were sharing a peak of joy and rapture it had suddenly been cut off and she was back to mundane reality. As she walked to her flat she felt like a puppet on a string, as if someone else were reponsible for her movements. Through the lighted windows of the canteen she could see nurses and doctors eating at plastic topped tables, or queuing at the counter with trays, and she realised that she was back in the world where she belonged. Sami would go back to his hotel. His hotel? Once again she had no idea where he was staying. In fact, she reflected, there was very little that she did know about him.

CHAPTER FIVE

A WEEK passed and then another and Zena realised sadly that she might never see Sami again. At first her heart had lifted hopefully whenever she took an outside telephone call. She hoped for a letter or a message but there was nothing. She had no idea if he was still in England. Every detail of their last meeting was sharp and clear in her mind. The way he had held her close to him; the masculinity of his body; his mouth on hers and the brush of his moustache against her cheek. With infinite shame she remembered how eagerly she had responded to his kisses. How incredibly naïve of her to have believed him when he told her that he loved her. Thank goodness the taxi-driver had spoken when he did, thereby saving her from further folly. He might even be married and have a family, but she had given that possibility no thought at all although she knew so little about him. Was it because she was twenty-six and love-starved . . . or sex-starved . . . that she had fallen so easily for his charm, his doubtless oft-repeated words of love?

Suddenly everything became heart-wrenchingly clear. He was married, of course he was! That was why he had refused to answer her when she asked him if there was a cousin lined up for him to marry. Had he told her he already had a wife it would have cramped his style later in the evening. Something stirred in the back of her mind. Somewhere she had read that Arabs took mistresses when they were abroad as a matter of course. And not only Arabs, she thought bitterly. There was something to be said for having a career instead of marriage. Although at times she felt her heart was bruised and aching with loneliness, on the whole she found her work satisfying and full of interest and it did not let you down as a man could.

So now she settled back to her normal routine of admittances, operations, post-operative problems and staffing difficulties. She scraped her hair even farther behind her ears and adopted a more commanding manner in her determination not to act as a silly love-sick teenager. Student nurses kept clear of her as much as possible, patients paused in their shouted conversations and fell silent when she entered the ward, and Sue suggested it was time she took a holiday.

The amount of paper-work seemed to grow and grow, so that sometimes Zena had the feeling that she would be discovered one day buried under a mountain of it. The trouble was that no sooner did she get started on settling a query than the telephone would ring, disturbing her concentration and needing some immediate action on her part, so that when she came back to her original job she had to go through all the preliminaries again. She had had a particularly frustrating day and, when the telephone gave its initial single ring before starting to peal in earnest, she looked at it with loathing and was tempted to ignore it, but knew it was impossible. When at last she snatched up the receiver it was the operator who said she had an outside call for her. There was a clicking sound and then the velvety-soft voice she had given up all hope of hearing again and had tried to forget, sounded so near that she could almost imagine he was in the room with her.

Although her heart was pounding with excitement she kept her voice cool as she said, 'Well, hello, Sami. I thought you had returned home long ago. How are you?'

'Thanks be to God I am well. And I am home, calling you from Kuwait.'

'Kuwait? Then what can I do for you?'

'You can just speak to me and let me hear your voice, Zena.'

Did he know what this call would cost him? 'What do you want, Sami?' She spoke hurriedly.

'What do I want? Can't you guess, Zena? What I want is you.'

A trolley clattered past her door and there was a sudden burst of conversation from a couple of nurses. Zena thought she had heard what he said, but it might have been her imagination. 'Sorry, I didn't catch that. What did you say?'

His voice was deep and vibrant with feeling. 'I said I want you.'

A knot of bitterness tightened inside her. So he admitted blatantly that he wanted her. He didn't love her, he wanted her, she was just a sex object to him and he had doubtless felt cheated, as she had, by the taxi-driver's intervention.

'So you want me, do you?' she said cuttingly. 'And I want my own helicopter.'

There was a silence which was long enough for Zena to regret her sharp rejoinder. 'Then you shall have one, my darling, if you become my wife.'

She opened her mouth to make some reply but no words came.

'Did you hear me, Zena?' he asked anxiously.

'Yes. I . . . I heard what you said, but you were joking. What is it you rang up about?'

His voice became unbelievably harsh. 'You imagine I would joke about such a matter?'

'I don't know. I mean . . . what am I supposed to say? Are you asking me to marry you?' No sooner had she said the words than she wished she could recall them. Of course he had not meant that.

'That is why I have rung you, Zena. Just say that you love me and the rest will be simple.'

There was a buzzing in her head and a pulse beat so strongly in her throat that she felt she was choking. Marry Sami? Marry him? Did she even love him? She liked his company and his attentions, and she liked . . . no, loved being close to him. But marry him? She recalled the sensuous thrill of being in his arms, the deep down emotions it had stirred in her, feelings that she had never before experienced. But marry him? Why, she scarcely knew him.

'Zena, are you there? Did you hear me?'

'Yes,' she whispered.

'Then will you please give me your answer?' His voice, although pleading, was insistent.

'Oh Sami, how can I? Answer you, I mean. You ask me such an important thing out of the blue and expect an answer immediately. And over the telephone.'

He spoke slowly as if he was having difficulty over finding the right words. 'I will try and explain, Zena, try to get you to understand. When I returned home I expected to forget you. I hoped very much that I would be able to do that because it would be much simpler for me and save a lot of problems. But I cannot do that. And what about you, Zena? Had you forgotten me? Has another patient taken my place in your heart?'

'No,' Zena said truthfully. 'I have thought about you every day. When I didn't hear from you I felt very hurt.'

'Then marry me, Zena. I want to spend my life with you. I want to grow old with you.' His voice, full of emotion, suddenly sounded more foreign than she remembered.

She felt trapped as if she was a prisoner in a glorious glass room lit by sunlight, but try as she would she could find no way out of it. Frantically she tried to think of something to say that would postpone the necessity of making a decision. 'But your father,' she said, feeling as if she was clutching at a hitherto unseen door handle. 'Wouldn't he prefer you to marry a Kuwaiti?'

There was a pause, and, knowing how sensitive he was, she feared that she had offended him. 'You . . . you told me it was usual for first cousins to marry . . .'

In the silence that ensued it was almost as if, over the telephone wire, she felt him stiffen. Then he spoke hesitantly. 'That is true, Zena, my father will not be pleased, but that is only natural and to be expected. But when he sees you and knows how much we love one another, if it is God's will he will give his consent.'

And if it is not His will, what then? Zena wondered in alarm. I would have given up my work and my country for nothing. 'Sami,' she said gently. 'I do love you . . . in a way . . . but marriage is something more . . . it is so important . . . so lasting . . . at least it would be for me.'

'You think it would not be for me also?' His voice rose indignantly.

She chose her words with care. 'If you married the right person I am sure it would be. But I still believe that what you feel for me is not the love which leads to marriage. I happened to be there when you needed someone—any sympathetic woman would have served the purpose. This frequently happens, you know. Patients imagine they have fallen in love with their doctor or nurse, but it doesn't last; nobody expects it to.'

His voice was stern and held a tinge of rebuke. 'I am not a child, Zena, but a man with serious intentions. In all my life I have not wanted to marry until now and I am quite sure of my feelings.'

'But Sami . . .' Her voice trembled. 'I . . . I am not sure that I love you in the same way . . .'

'Then I will teach you to do so. I will return immediately and bring you back to Kuwait so that you may meet my family. I will be with you in a week.'

Terrified that he would replace the receiver and that her future would be mapped out irretrievably she cried hastily, 'No, Sami, no. I need time to think about it. I will write to you, I promise.'

'Then make it soon or I will come to England and get my answer in person. And I will not take "no" for an answer.' He said the words lightly but underneath them she sensed a definite threat which caused her to shiver involuntarily.

When he had rung off and she had replaced the receiver she sat staring into space waiting to let her mind absorb his words. What is the matter with me? she asked herself. If someone had told her only half an hour ago that Sami would propose marriage to her she would have been over the moon with delight. Why else had she been behaving so abominably because she had not heard from him? She loved him. She wanted him. But . . . A cautionary inner voice reminded her that nothing had changed, she still did not know anything about him. But that is why he wants you to go to Kuwait to find out, her mind replied. Her thoughts swung this way and that as she tried to come to a decision, and all the while the telephone kept ringing demanding her attention, and for once she was glad to shelve her own problem if only temporarily.

The days passed during which time she pushed the need for making a decision to the back of her mind, until she suddenly became alarmed, believing that if she did not soon give Sami his answer he would return as he had warned her. In any event it was not fair of her to keep him on tenter-hooks; she must write him a kind letter to soften the disappointment of her refusal. Her refusal? At the thought something beautiful and romantic seemed to fade, leaving her with the stark reality of the scuffed and battered Edgewarebury Hospital for the rest of her life, punctuated by a visit to Knightsbridge on her day off. Nevertheless, time and again she started the letter, until her wastepaper basket was filled to overflowing with crumpled rejects. She reminded herself once more that he would come back and then she would be lost. Lost? What a strange word to use. It would be marvellous for him to make his decision for her, wonderful to agree to his plans and just follow wheresoever he led. Then that inner voice started arguing again. To Kuwait? To a country she knew nothing about? Where she would be a foreigner away from all her friends and relations and unable to speak the language? . . . To be married to Sami?

She was unable to sleep and had to resort to the sleeping pills which she handed out to patients, yet even so she tossed and turned throughout the nights in a ferment of indecision. There was the terrifying fear of the finality of committing herself to Sami for life, warring with the knowledge that not to do so was like shutting out all the colour and warmth and leaving herself in a dull, grey mundane world. This was not a thing that could be decided so hurriedly, she needed time and other surroundings. She must go away, if only temporarily, away from the same drabness of the hospital and out of Sami's glamorous reach. No sooner had she come to this decision than she was impatient to do something about it. The journal in which vacancies were advertised was late in coming out, due to an industrial dispute, but sometimes the latest available 'vacancies' were pinned on the staff notice-board. She had a quick look around the ward and asked Sue to answer the telephone while she was gone. Then she took the lift to the ground floor and threaded her way along the corridors which were busy with doctors, patients and nurses, and porters wheeling trolleys to and from the wards and X-ray department.

Her eyes roamed over the board, skimming through the notices which referred to forthcoming productions by the Drama Society; badminton and table tennis fixtures; a union meeting; articles found or lost; holiday addresses, and second-hand goods for sale. Then, as she was about to walk despondently away, she caught sight of a neatly typed card: 'Nursing staff required on a 1, 2 or 3 year contract in Kuwait. For application forms please ring . . .'

Someone was playing a joke on her. Sue? No, she didn't really believe that. But how fortuitous, how coincidental! She looked hastily over her shoulder almost expecting Sami to be there watching her as he had done at Knightsbridge Station. She jotted down the telephone number, and as she walked away every nerve in her body was alert for the feel of his hand on her shoulder, his voice in her ear. When she reached her office she sank on to her chair dazed with relief. This was the obvious, heaven-sent solution; it was exactly what she needed, to be able to visit Kuwait as a free person, to see the country and Sami in his own surroundings.

When the application forms arrived, Zena filled them in immediately and took them to Miss Simms, the senior nursing officer. Miss Simms was surprisingly young; so that Zena knew that, if she stayed on at Edgwarebury Hospital, the chances of herself reaching that exalted status, before she was too old to care, were remote. She was a large, raw-boned woman who looked at Zena through the lenses that made her eyes appear enormous.

'I would like to apply for this vacancy, ma'am, if you would be willing to grant me one year's leave,' Zena said, certain that it would be sufficient time for her to find out what she wanted to know.

She raised her head like a tortoise looking out from its shell. 'So you wish to go to Kuwait. Do you know anything about that country, Sister?'

'No, I don't. I know it is a state on the Persian Gulf, but that's about all.'

'Mmmm? So what makes you think you want to go there? If you expect your application to have my blessing you must tell me some more.'

Zena hesitated. She knew that if she mentioned the true reason, in no way would Miss Simms agree. Falling in love with, or becoming involved with, a patient was completely taboo. Indeed Miss Simms would not begin to understand and as Zena looked at her something tightened inside her. Did she want to stay here and grow like her?

'I am very happy here, Miss Simms, and proud of my appointment as Ward Sister, but I feel I would like to gain more experience, see something of the world while I am still young enough to enjoy it and benefit from it. I have never been abroad and this seemed a wonderful opportunity.'

Miss Simms squeezed her cheeks and rubbed her hand across her mouth. 'There are other places, other vacancies that arise from time to time that you'd probably enjoy more. Kuwait is a very hot country, very hot indeed. Starting around now the temperature is anything between 112° and 120° and you might find the conditions very trying.'

'Yes ma'am, but I'm tougher than I look, I think I

would be able to cope. And it is now that I want to go for
. . . for personal reasons.' Hastily she added, 'And if I
may, I would like a week's leave immediately so that I
can go home to visit my parents.'

Miss Simms looked at her inquisitively as she rested
her chin on her fist, and Zena's heart sank. But suddenly
the telephone rang and as she reached for the receiver,
she said, 'Very well, I'll see what I can do. You can take
your leave and if you leave the forms with me—have you
filled them in?—then I will send them off with my
reference.'

The following day Zena travelled down to Penzance on
the Cornish Riviera. When Sue heard that Zena was
taking a week's leave, she heaved a sigh of relief.

'Thank heavens for that! Now perhaps we can all be
the happy fun-loving crowd we were before you started
heading for this nervous breakdown,' she said cheerfully.

'Nervous breakdown, my foot! I just need a holiday.'
Zena decided not to mention the fact that she had
applied for the transfer to Kuwait, in case nothing came
of it, and if she had told Sue it would be equivalent to
announcing it over the loudspeaker.

She thought for a long time, then sent Sami a cable
saying she would be away for a week and would write or
phone him when she returned, for she did not want to
risk him arriving at the hospital enquiring for her. She
had telephoned her parents that she was coming down
on a week's leave, but even so she guessed that they
would suspect that there was some reason for her unexpected visit.

When she reached Penzance she decided against taking a bus or taxi, and instead walked along the promenade to her home. It was somewhat early in the year for
many visitors to have descended on the town, and the
people who sat on the seats or in the shelters were
elderly local people or mothers with young children. The
bay was calm and sun-dappled and St Michael's Mount

looked as it always did, beautiful, impressive and eternal. She leaned on the promenade railings and looked down on the pebbles and rocks draped with seaweed, and across to the crater in the headland which was the Newlyn quarry, and a part of her wished she had never left Cornwall where everything seemed so peaceful and placid. She closed her eyes and let the breeze ruffle her hair as she listened to the gently moving waves sucking at the shingle and the perpetual crying of the seagulls.

There was a savoury smell coming from the kitchen when she reached home, and Jock, the Scottie, with his doggy sense had seemed to know just when she reached the corner of the road, for he set up a frenzied barking. It was good to be home! It was great to be on holiday, to be able to get up as late as she liked, to go for walks with Jock, and into the town with her mother. It was after she had been there several days that she plucked up the courage to mention the possibility of her going to Kuwait.

'Kuwait? What do you want to go there for?' her mother asked, her eyes looking shocked.

'Just for a change. I'm a bit fed-up with being in Edgwarebury Hospital.'

Her mother looked at her suspiciously. 'But you've only just been made a Sister; it would be a pity to leave now.'

'I know but . . . I'd like to see a bit of the world . . .'

'You want to do what I did, go out on the district, you wouldn't get bored with that, it's a lovely life. You meet so many people and you travel around the countryside. If you could get down here, look how nice that would be.'

'Yes it would, but not now. Maybe later on. Just now I would like to go abroad . . . only for a time . . . just for a year . . .' Her heart gave a sudden throb of pain as she realised that if she married Sami she would be gone for more than a year; it would be for ever.

Jock made a funny little whinnying sound in his throat, and staggering up on his hind legs licked Zena's face with his agitated tongue. She rubbed her head against his hairy coat, and when she could control her voice she said, too brightly, 'Kuwait is not the end of the world. Some of our patients ring up from there quite frequently to enquire this or that.'

Her father materialised from nowhere and stood by the kitchen door. 'Kuwait? It'd be a fine experience for you to see what it's like over there. It's a very wealthy country now, you know, with all this oil they've got. I've heard that their schools and their hospitals, too, are the last word with all the best equipment and air-conditioning, so the heat wouldn't bother you too much.'

Zena struggled in her mind to find some opening remark, some way of telling them about Sami. It seemed very secretive not to do so, and yet she knew that if she did her mother would worry, maybe unnecessarily. She was debating what to say when her mother said warningly, 'Don't you go getting involved with any of those oil-sheikhs; they'll have their eye on you, you may depend, you being so fair.'

Zena smiled a stiff lop-sided smile that hurt the corners of her mouth. 'Oil-sheikh? And how do you think a poor working girl is going to meet one of those? Anyhow, it's all pie in the sky. I've only applied for the vacancy and I don't suppose for a moment that I'll get it.'

But on the day she returned to work Miss Simms sent for her and told her she had been accepted. 'You will leave in a fortnight's time. It is very inconvenient having to replace you at such short notice but I have made enquiries and am fortunate in getting a temporary replacement. She will, of course, have your flat, so lock away any of your personal things, then she will know what she can use.'

'Thank you, Miss Simms, I am very grateful for your help.'

'Here is a list of the injections you will need to have.' She passed Zena a sheet of paper. 'I rely on you to have full information on your patients and procedures to

Sister Ping who will be replacing you, and introduce her to your staff. In case I don't see you again I wish you well. And remember, you are an English nurse and, as such, an ambassador of this country, so be careful not to do anything that could bring your profession into disrepute. I am sure I have no need to tell you that; everyone speaks highly of you.' She proffered a hard, dry hand.

When Sue heard Zena's news her red, good-natured face was a picture of dismay. 'Kuwait? What on earth do you want to go there for? It's practically desert and will be as hot as hell.'

Zena shrugged. 'It'll be a change. How come you know so much about it? I didn't even know where it was until I looked it up.'

'So why Kuwait?' Her voice was a crescendo of suspicion. 'Wait a minute . . . Isn't that where the brain-op chap came from? That Garibaldi? Don't tell me it's because of him that you're going there!'

Zena said with flat finality, 'His name is Gharbally, and yes, that is why I am going there.'

Sue slapped her forehead in despair. 'Now I've heard everything. For heaven's sake, Zena, don't be so crazy. Once he's got you over there you'll be at his mercy . . . they don't think anything of women, you know, especially Western ones.'

Fighting her dragging sense of uncertainty, Zena retorted, 'As a matter of fact he has asked me to marry him, so you've got hold of the wrong end of the stick.' Immediately she had spoken she was furious with herself for not keeping it a secret.

Sue's mouth dropped open. 'Marry him!! Marry him!! You wouldn't do that. Of course, he fancies you because he's not used to fair girls. Once he got over the novelty it would be a different cup of tea.'

'Who's to say? And anyhow, isn't that what marriage is all about? Someone fancying someone else?'

'It's all very well to fancy someone but you must know as well as I do that their ways, their customs, their religion—they're great on that—they pray five times a day!—it's all so different from ours. Don't do it, Zena.' She laid her hand persuasively on her shoulder.

A smothering sense of frustration swept over Zena and she covered her face with her hands. 'Oh Sue, now you've made me undecided all over again,' she said miserably.

'The very fact that you are so undecided must mean that it's wrong. Honestly, Zena, you would be as wrong for him as he would for you. Anyhow, why the rush? He's only been gone a few weeks.'

'He wanted an answer, one way or the other, immediately. I couldn't say "no" and I was too scared to say "yes",' Zena admitted. 'So I thought, if only I could get away somewhere and give myself time to think it over. I'd imagined going to Newcastle or Oxford or somewhere like that, but when I looked at the board there was this thing about vacancies in Kuwait and it seemed like fate, and I applied for it on the spur of the moment.'

'And got it, of course, because nobody else would want to go there, you may depend.'

Zena looked at her appealingly. 'Don't you think it's a good idea though? For me to be able to see the country and Sami's home without committing myself?'

'If you take my advice you'll say "No" loudly and clearly in as many languages as you know, right now,' Sue said emphatically. 'But nobody ever does take advice, especially when it is good.'

'Sue,' Zena said eagerly. 'What about you coming too? Wouldn't that be great?'

Sue shook her head slowly and determinedly. 'No thank you, it's the last thing I want to do. Quite apart from the fact that I couldn't bear to see you making a fool of yourself, I don't think Miss Simms would take kindly to losing both of us.' She pushed herself up from her chair, and as she moved towards the door her expression changed from impatience to affection.

'Please don't do anything daft, love. Maybe you fancy

this chap, but there will be others for sure. And if they don't appeal to you, you could have a great future in nursing, you know; you're a clever girl.'

Zena stared at the closed door and suddenly she knew with certainty that, although she was marginally better in examinations than Sue, when it came to ordinary common-sense she was not in the same class as her friend.

CHAPTER SIX

WHEN the plane touched down at Kuwait Airport Zena looked apprehensively around but was reassured to see that it could as easily have been Heathrow. Taking her hand baggage from the rack she followed the other passengers down the two flights of steps leading from the aircraft to the tarmac, and made her way to the airport buildings. After clearing Passport Control, she collected her suitcases and went through Customs to get a taxi. She had been assured by the clerk in the travel agency that this would present no difficulty, but the hordes of pushing passengers milling around, all equally eager for transport, gave the lie to that statement. She stood in the blistering heat wondering how long she would have to wait, when she saw a vaguely familiar figure noticeable even in that crowded area. He stood taller than most and looked disturbingly attractive in a short sleeved cream shirt over dark pants with light brown hair falling over his forehead, and dark-browed eyes that scanned the crowd. Her heart leapt at the sight. What on earth was the typically British Mr Smythe doing here? As she stared at him in fascinated amazement he raised his hand in a greeting. Embarrassed in case he should imagine she thought he was greeting her she turned away and stared fixedly at nothing in particular.

Suddenly there was a movement beside her and she swung around to see her suitcases being whisked up off the ground.

'Come along,' Mr Smythe said tersely.

Zena stood where she was, her back rigid. 'It's all right, thank you. I am waiting for a taxi,' she said coolly, tilting her chin so that her hair swung away from her cheeks.

'For goodness' sake! It's too hot to stand here arguing. Anyhow, you'd have a very long wait; taxis are snapped up on sight, you don't just stand there.' He opened the door of a small blue car. 'Will you get in?' He sounded exasperated, and meeting the grey thrust of his eyes she obeyed him, afraid that if she hesitated he would lose patience and go without her. He stowed her cases in the boot then walked around the car to slide in beside her. He inserted his key in the ignition, the engine hummed into life and with practised skill he manoeuvred his way in and out of the maelstrom of cars that seemed to follow no rule of the road.

Once they were clear of the airport Zena said, 'What a surprise seeing you here.'

'And what is so surprising about that?' he asked casually, his eyes on the road ahead.

She felt a spurt of anger. What a stupid reply; it was as if he liked being difficult. She had no doubt it was second nature to him.

'Well,' she said with a faint note of irony, 'this isn't exactly Edgwarebury or even London. One doesn't expect to meet someone one knows. It is quite a few miles from home.'

A derisive smile twisted the corners of his mouth. 'Oh, come now, you knew that I was here.'

'I knew?' Oh he was insufferable! This conceited creature was capable of imagining she had come here because of him, she did believe. 'I knew?' she repeated, her voice rising. 'Of course I didn't know. Why should I have?'

He rested his elbow on the window ledge and turned his face towards her. His eyes mocked her and looked at her with utter disbelief. 'You sent in your application to me, remember?'

Zena took in a huge breath and exhaled it in a gasp of fury. 'To you? I did nothing of the kind. I wouldn't have . . Oh!' she faltered, suddenly shocked with the memory.

He raised an eyebrow. 'And what does "Oh" mean?'

'Well,' she said, twisting her hands together, 'I've just remembered. I didn't send it anywhere. I left it with Miss Simms and she said she would send it off with her recommendation. I had no idea you would be here, honestly, or . . .'

He interrupted her with a smile. 'Or you would not have come I suppose.'

A wave of colour ran up into her cheeks. 'It wouldn't have made any difference,' she said angrily. Then, ashamed that she was behaving so badly to him when he was doing her a favour in meeting her, she slewed around and gazed out of the window at the passing scene.

There were many multi-storeyed glass and concrete buildings, the dual carriage-way was jam-packed with vehicles, and the pavements were crowded with pedestrians. It could have been a big, modern city almost anywhere in the world.

'Why did you choose to come here?' The voice beside her asked lazily.

There was a moment of silence while Zena decided what reply to make, for she had not the slightest intention of telling him the real reason. She chewed her thumb reflectively. 'I felt that I wanted a real change, to get away. I think it does people good to get away from the day to day routine, don't you?'

He nodded. 'Certainly it does. But why Kuwait?'

'That was just by chance. I wanted to get away from Edgwarebury for a time—not to go to Cornwall which is my home that I love, but somewhere quite different. I happened to see this vacancy on the notice board.' She gave a little laugh. 'I think I would have applied for any vacancy at all, but this happened to be the only one. Why have you come here?'

'That was quite a surprise too. Apparently some wealthy Kuwaiti made the suggestion to the hospital board of governors and they made me a very tempting offer. The money alone would not have persuaded me but I thought it would be interesting. However I wanted

English nurses around me and thought the quickest way of getting them was to put notices on the boards of our group of hospitals.'

Zena felt a rush of pleasure to realise that other English nurses would be here too. 'How many nurses are coming?' she asked eagerly.

He shrugged his wide shoulders. 'I managed to persuade Sister Bolitho from St Stephen's to come along. I was very pleased about that because she is first-rate and I should be completely lost without her. But nobody else wanted to know.'

'When did Sister Bolitho arrive?'

'Unfortunately she couldn't get away just yet; they couldn't spare her. But she will be here in due course. That will make the three of us.'

Once again, Zena thought, with an inner grimace, you are putting me in my place. You knew perfectly well that when I applied for leave it was given immediately, almost as if they were glad to be rid of me, but apparently Sister Bolitho is something more special. 'I am surprised,' she said drily, 'that you were unable to persuade more nurses to accompany you. Such a wonderful opportunity!' She gave him a quick look from under her lashes.

He eyed her speculatively. 'Kuwait is not exactly a pleasure resort; it is not a pretty spot, it is very hot, extremely busy and on the edge of the desert. It is not a place for tourists; indeed they are discouraged. I can't help feeling that any nurse who comes here must have an ulterior motive.'

Something inside her tightened and as she stared woodenly ahead she prayed that he would not press the point. After a while he said, glancing at her fair hair and skin, 'You will have to take great care at first not to go out in the sun too much; wait until you gradually become accustomed to it. You will find it quite comfortable working in the hospital, however, because of the excellent air-conditioning.'

She wrinkled her nose at him, and said flippantly, 'In

other words don't expect any time off, we are only thinking of your own good.'

'We are thinking of everyone's good. We don't want our staff on the sick list.'

He drove into the hospital grounds and Zena was surprised at the size of the building. It was very white and very modern with windows which made it appear like an office block. It was set in a vast courtyard which was bordered on three sides by single-storeyed buildings, and it was outside one of these that he stopped the car. He nodded towards it. 'This bungalow is going to be your home for the next twelve months. What do you think of it?'

A striped awning shaded the windows and door and on the sills were boxes gay with flowers. 'Will it be all mine?' she asked, her eyes widening.

He felt in his pocket and produced a key. 'Your very own. Come on, let's see what it's like inside.'

Zena stepped out of the car and was immediately hit by the oven-like heat. She looked at the other bungalows. 'Are these for the other nurses?'

'Yes, for those who need them. Some, of course, live out.' He glanced across at the hospital. 'It's rather a beauty, don't you think?'

She shook her head. 'It doesn't look like a hospital to me, I'm so used to Edgwarebury with its old dark bricks and chimneys. Is this one as modern and hygienic inside as it is out?'

He nodded. 'It certainly is; you can't fault it; it's a joy to work in. Now—do I carry you over the threshold?' He looked at her with a smile deep down in his eyes.

'No, you jolly well don't,' she laughed. 'That is a new husband's privilege. I will go in on my own two feet.'

Zena was delighted by the coolness of the bungalow, thanks to the shaded windows and the tiled floors. It was larger than her flatlet in Edgwarebury, having a bedroom in addition to the living room and a large luxurious bathroom. There was a minimum of furniture, but everything she needed, and an earlier occupant had left a

few brightly coloured prints hanging on the walls, and an
ornament or two. Theodore Smythe looked around
critically, one hand deep in his pocket. 'It's a bit spartan
but a darned sight better than what we had at St
Stephen's. Are you pleased with it?'

Zena smiled her approval. 'The best part about it is
having it all to myself, bathroom and all, although I was
proud of my little flatlet. I didn't imagine that you would
live in at St Stephen's.'

'I didn't, I had my flat in Harley Street, but I've seen
Sister Bolitho's accommodation, and it isn't very
wonderful.' He glanced at his watch and frowned. 'I
should have liked to have been able to show you around
but I have an appointment.' He beckoned her towards
the door and pointed to a building at the far end of the
courtyard. 'That is the canteen and beyond it is a lounge
and recreation room. Up on the roof there is a very nice
garden which you might enjoy if you find it too hot down
below. Now, when you have unpacked, I should go
along to the canteen and get something to eat and
drink.'

'What is the food like? Typically canteen?'

'Inevitably,' he replied. 'More oily than back home
but you will have to come to terms with that. Right. Well
I hope you will settle in here OK and be happy.'

She smiled up at him, her eyes startlingly blue in the
pale oval of her face, as she longed to show her apprecia-
tion of his company after her initial hostility. 'Thank you
so much, Mr Smythe, for meeting me and bringing me
here; it was awfully kind of you. I should have felt
completely lost on my own.'

'And that would never do, would it?' He sketched a
small salute. 'I'll be seeing you, Zena.'

When he had gone a smile still lifted the corners of her
mouth as she savoured again the fact that he had called
her by her Christian name. She wondered how many
years it would have taken in England for him to have got
around to doing that, and she guessed that it would
never have happened. She flopped in a chair and closed

her eyes and the surprising knowledge came to her that
Mr Smythe had turned out to be quite a pleasant man.

Work in the hospital was similar to that in Edgwarebury,
illness and its treatment being the same the world over.
The wards were spacious and held twelve beds each.
Every piece of furniture and equipment was the finest
that money could buy and to Zena's surprise everything
was free for Kuwaitis and for non-Kuwaitis if they were
in government service. There were just a few private
suites of unbelievable luxury for the wealthiest Arabs,
the oil-sheikhs and their families who wished to pay.

She discovered that she was in charge of a ward and
she was surprised yet thankful, for it would have entailed
a great deal of responsibility and many problems, not the
least of which would have been the language barrier.
The other nurses were of many nationalities rather than
Kuwaiti, and all had some knowledge of the English
language, although it was limited, but it made her feel
guiltily aware that she was at a disadvantage knowing
nothing of theirs. She was glad beyond words to know
that Mr Symthe was near at hand even though she never
saw him, for without the knowledge that he was in the
vicinity she would have felt overwhelmingly lonely, a
stranger in a strange land. Now that she was here she was
amazed at her impetuosity in coming here on the
strength of knowing just Sami. Sami? She had not yet got
in touch with him for she wanted time to adjust to her
new surroundings, and she was not yet ready to think
about her future and what part he might play in it.

On a sweltering afternoon when she had come off duty
she decided to seek the coolness of the roof garden.
There were ornamental iron chairs set out under huge
awnings, and potted plants and flowers trailed over the
walls and floor making vivid splashes of colour. She
leaned on the coping of the parapet and looked out over
the city. There were streets of office blocks, tall buildings, their many windows dazzling her with the reflected
sunlight, and over on the skyline were domed mosques

with slender minarets. The streets were thronged with cars and men and women going about their business. She felt she was looking on the scene from another world and suddenly she had an inexplicable feeling of panic, and despite the heat of the day she shivered and longed to get back inside the building.

When she stepped out of the lift on the ground floor she stood for a moment damp with perspiration caused not entirely by the heat, and leaned against a wall. People of all nationalities glided past her and she had a great longing to be back in Edgwarebury Hospital where she knew practically every employee and was known and respected by them. Her mouth went dry as she thought of the year that stretched ahead of her and tears pricked her eyelids. She blinked hard and as her eyes cleared she saw a door opposite suddenly open and a man come out. Through the open door she glimpsed Mr Smythe's tall figure wearing a green gown, his face half-covered by a mask. Without pausing to think she moved quickly towards him. 'Mr Smythe,' she called, and with a tight feeling in her throat wondered what she could say next. She just had a deep-down longing to speak to someone from home.

He looked swiftly round, only his grey eyes were visible between his cap and his mask. She ran her tongue over her dry lips and said the only thing she could think of. 'Hello.'

Pulling his cap off he shook his hair free then removed his mask and came out to join her. 'Hello to you. How are you getting along?'

'Oh . . . fine. I . . . I'm off duty now and I was just wandering around.'

'Why don't you go up on the roof?'

'I've just come down. When I saw you . . . I . . . I'm sorry, I shouldn't have called you, but . . . but it was so lovely to see someone familiar.' To her horror she heard her voice crack.

As he looked down at her from his great height his eyes were warm and compassionate. 'I do believe you

are feeling homesick! Never mind, we all have suffered
from it at one time or another.'

'Really? She could not believe that he would ever feel
as she was feeling at this moment; he was far too
self-sufficient and confident.'

He appeared to be considering something, then he
said, 'Look, I've finished here now. Just give me a while
to shower and get a sandwich, and I'll show you around
the town if you would like that.'

Gratitude and pleasure surged up inside her so strongly that she had an overwhelming urge to throw her arms
around him. A quick smile lit her face as she pictured his
reaction if she gave way to the impulse. 'How very kind
of you, that would be marvellous,' she said.

'Righto, I'll pick you up in about an hour.' He
vanished inside the room again.

Zena had a long cool bath and chose to wear a
primrose coloured cotton dress which was nothing more
than two pieces of material with a frill at the hemline and
joined at the sides and on the shoulders. It had been the
only dress made of cotton that she had been able to buy
in Edgwarebury, and she had thought the price staggering considering that it was so simple. She brushed her
hair and let it swing free, then stared at herself in the
mirror. Her eyes looked incredulously back at her as she
told herself that she was going out with Mr Smythe, and
more than that, she was delighted to be doing so. She
searched back in her mind trying to recall what she had
ever found objectionable about him, but could not at
first recall. Oh yes, he had snubbed her at their first
meeting and criticised her attitude at their second, but in
retrospect she believed she had deserved it on both
occasions. And he had more than made up for it since
by, first of all, meeting her off the plane and now,
although he had no need to, was going to show her the
town. He had proved to be what everybody else had
said, a very charming man.

Her conversation with herself came to an abrupt end
as the subject of it arrived in person and rang her bell.

His hair was damp from his shower and his teeth gleamed white against his sun-tanned skin. He nodded his approval as he looked around the bungalow. 'Now it looks better, more lived in. Is it quite comfortable?'

'Oh yes, it's all anyone needs; I like it very much.'

'And the canteen? How do you like the food?'

'I can't say that I enjoy it very much, but does one ever like canteen food?' she asked, tilting her head to one side.

'No, we've swopped sausages and baked beans for mutton and rice cooked in oceans of oil. By the time we return to England we will no doubt be grossly over-weight.' His eyes travelled slowly over her. 'You've got a good way to go before you qualify as a stout lady. Now shall we go by car or walk? It isn't far but it will be hot.'

'I'd rather walk please, if it's all right with you.'

As they made their way through the hospital grounds Zena took stock of him. He was tall and lean and muscular in an open-necked, short sleeved shirt over light mohair slacks. The sun on his arms and chest turned the hairs on them to gold. She glimpsed the strong square line of his jaw, the determined mouth and the brown hair that had grown a little longer around his neck and ears.

Suddenly he looked down at her. 'Why are you staring at me?'

'I—I was thinking that only mad dogs and Englishmen go out in the mid-day sun and I wondered if we would get sunstroke or something,' she said on the spur of the moment.

'Sister Foster,' he said reprovingly, 'how very unpro-fessional of you! What exactly would the "or something" be? In any event it is not mid-day and we are both English, thank God.'

Zena scarcely listened for she felt hurt and dis-appointed that he had reverted to calling her Sister Foster when previously it had been Zena.

He appeared to know exactly where they were going and she wondered at that. 'Have you been to Kuwait before?' she asked.

'Of course,' he replied blandly. 'When I was invited to come here I wanted to see what I would be letting myself in for, so naturally I came over to look around.'

Naturally you would, Zena thought. But it would never have entered my head to do that even if I could have afforded to.

'And you decided that you liked it?'

He shrugged. 'I liked the hospital and the knowledge that the best of equipment was mine for the asking, that there would be no pleading my case only to have it turned down because of the expense. That is a wonderful feeling. But as for liking Kuwait itself, that needs more thinking about. The original city would have pleased me more I think, the present one is too modernised for my liking although there are marvellous facilities and all of them free. It is a very wealthy state thanks to the oil, and I understand there is no tax on income.'

'How long have you come out for?'

'Initially for one year. I will see how things go, then maybe sign on for another year. Let me see, you are here for one year, aren't you?' He smiled disarmingly. 'And already wishing it was for just one month?'

She nodded. 'I expect I'll get used to it,' she said, confident that she was speaking the truth now that he was beside her. It was the loneliness she found hardest to contend with.

The town could almost have been in England or America with large stores stocked with European goods, western style clothes and boutiques with models dressed in the latest Parisian fashion. The signs over the doors were printed somewhat inexpertly in English. Everywhere there was brash neon lighting and much plate glass. Zena felt disappointed that after travelling so far she was seeing what she could have seen in any High Street in England and she was not sufficiently conversant with the currency to know how the prices compared.

'I'm sure that if I went into one of these stores I would imagine I was in England,' Zena said.

'I daresay. Most everything is the same everywhere

nowadays. It seems a great pity because visitors come to a country to see its culture; they want something different from back home, but the planners feel it necessary to provide them with what they are accustomed to, to make it a home from home.'

'I think it's quite heartbreaking. Even in Edgwarebury lovely old shops and houses have been pulled down to make way for high-rise blocks that have no character at all.'

'They've done it a lot in London, of course. Even the good old English breakfast has given way in many hotels to the Continental type.'

'And Chinese take-away or pizzas are taking the place of fish and chips.'

'It doesn't smell the same, does it? Nothing smells nicer on a cold night than frying fish.'

'Oh don't,' Zena protested, 'you're making me feel hungry.'

'Come on then, let's go in here.' He pushed open the door of a restaurant, but Zena hung back.

'I'm not really hungry. I couldn't eat anything now. It was just the thought of fish and chips,' she said.

'We'll have a drink then. Would you like coffee or something cooler?'

They had tall glasses of iced lemon decorated with slices of the fruit and mint leaves. Theodore stretched his long legs. 'It's good to sit down. You look as fresh as a flower but your legs are a lot younger than mine.'

Zena was immediately contrite. 'I had forgotten that you had just finished operating. You should have said and then we could have come by taxi. You must be very tired.'

'I'll survive. When we have finished this we'll go to the bazaar; I think you will find that more interesting.'

He hailed a taxi and as they drove away from the town centre, through a maze of twisting alley-ways, the atmosphere completely changed. Here all the Kuwaiti men were wearing traditional dress, the *dishdasha*, and the women, some of whom were veiled, wore long black cloaks. Now it certainly seemed to be another country. They dismissed the taxi and wandered around the bazaar. They were accosted on all sides by Indian shopkeepers, who, when they realised that their potential customers were Europeans, tried out their few words of English, urging them to buy at fantastically high prices. Zena was fascinated to see men sitting on the ground embroidering *abbas* with pure gold thread. She, however, was herself an object of curiosity and felt embarrassed by the bold stares from the men and moved closer to Theodore.

His eyes slanted down at her. 'I hope you feel suitably ashamed of being here on the streets in a state of undress, Zena?'

'Undress?' She looked down hastily at herself. 'I am not undressed.'

'You are by their standards, you know. As a western girl they imagine you must have loose morals, anyhow. To be decent you should be wearing a cloak and possibly a veil, at least to cover your head.'

'Should I really?' She looked up at him anxiously, her eyes darkly blue.

He touched her lightly under the chin with a long slender finger. 'Only if you were an Arab. As an English lady you can wear just whatever you like. Isn't that good to know?'

The bazaar was a whole area devoted to shopping, like a market with alcoves which were about ten feet wide, each piled with its own particular type of merchandise for shoppers to mull over, while the merchant sat outside. There was the bazaar which sold more variety of spices than Zena had ever heard of; another with tribal rugs which had been woven by Iraqi Badawi women; there were antiques and secondhand goods of no value jumbled together; hand-woven cloaks and a great deal of gold and silver jewellery.

'Before we go back I would like to buy some foodstuffs so that I can make myself a snack in my bungalow

Now you can enjoy all 12 latest Mills & Boon Romances every month. As a subscriber to our Reader Service, you'll receive all our new titles, delivered to your doorstep–postage and packing Free. There's no commitment–you can change your mind about subscribing at any time, but the 6 free books are yours to keep.

Take Six Books FREE!

That's right! Return the coupon now and your first parcel of books is absolutely Free. There are lots of other advantages–no hidden extra charges, a free monthly Newsletter, and our famous friendly service–'phone our editor Susan Welland now on 01-684 2141 if you have any queries.

You have nothing to lose–and a whole new world of Romance to gain. Fill in and post the coupon today–and send no money!

when I feel like it, instead of always going to the canteen,' Zena said. She bought eggs and fresh fruit in a supermarket, and decided that she would invite Theodore to share an omelette with her on their return.

The heat was blistering, almost unbearable and Zena's steps became slower. Theodore, after giving her a swift look of concern, hailed a taxi.

'We have walked farther than you realise, one always does on such trips. I thought you would enjoy seeing it all but maybe we should have spread it over a couple of trips. I'm sorry, I should have thought of it,' he said gently.

'Oh I've had a lovely time; I'll soon get over feeling tired. Better to be tired than bored. Thank you for giving up your time to me.' She eased her feet in her sandals.

'One day I'll take you to the harbour; it will be cooler there. And there is a good museum and also an artists' colony if you enjoy that kind of thing.'

So there was going to be a next time! She smiled at him gratefully. 'I shall look forward to that very much,' she said.

The taxi dropped them at the hospital gates and as they got out another cab which was following theirs braked hard and stopped. The window was wound down and a high, cultured voice cried, 'Hello Theodore, darling.'

They both turned around. 'Beryl!' Theodore cried delightedly and strode across to her. The woman climbed from the taxi and held her face up to be kissed. Theodore spoke to the driver and directed him to a bungalow at the far side of the courtyard, then came back to Beryl. 'Why didn't you let me know you were coming? I would have met you but I didn't expect you until next week.' He put his arm lightly around her.

'There was some talk of an airport strike later in the week so I insisted on leaving now. I told them that you were in urgent need of me. Are you?'

Theodore laughed, his eyes crinkling, with amusement. 'Am I in need of you? Of course I am.' He paused, then added straight-faced, 'You mean, of course, in the theatre?'

'I mean, of course, nothing of the kind,' she replied, her eyes caressing his face.

He turned to Zena to make the introductions. 'This is Sister Bolitho whom I told you about. Beryl, this is Zena Foster from Edgewarebury Hospital who is here to make up our trilogy.'

Beryl Bolitho was a large, imposing young woman, not over-tall nor over-fat, but big enough to look important. She held her head high so that she seemed to be looking down on the world in general. She could not be described as pretty; the most that could be said of her was that she was a fine figure of a woman with her straight back and high bosom. Her most striking feature was her hair which was set in deep waves and was a shade of reddish-copper. It was so brilliant that it was impossible to ignore it and Zena somewhat unkindly found herself wondering whether it was a wig. Her round green eyes like unripe gooseberries stared at Zena, in such a way that she felt she needed to brush her hair or powder her face or change her dress, or all three.

But she smiled and held out her hand. 'I hope you had a pleasant journey. I can't tell you how pleased I am that I won't be the only English nurse out here.'

'Are you? Personally I have always found that a good nurse is a good nurse, and I don't give a fig for her nationality. At Stephen's we have them from all over the world.' She turned to Theodore, her body successfully excluding Zena. 'Tell me, Theo, am I going to like it here? Is it a good hospital?'

'I'm sure you will appreciate the fact that everything money can buy is yours for the asking. Yes, you will probably like it very much.'

'What about the work? Are there any interesting cases at the moment?'

'No, just run of the mill. A word of warning, Beryl, my dear. Most of the patients are dead keen on talking about their symptoms. If you allow them, they will continue non-stop,' he grinned.

Beryl slipped her arm through his. 'I'm looking forward to it all very much. But just now I'm dying for a cup of tea. I hope they make it properly.'

'Do have some with me,' Zena offered. 'We have just been to the shops so I have everything that's needed. My bungalow is just over there.'

Beryl's eyes flickered. 'Thanks all the same but I want to make sure that the taxi driver leaves all my cases in my bungalow. And I must have a bath, I feel a mess.'

'Of course, I know just how it is after that journey.' Then turning to Theodore she said, 'You will come in, won't you?'

Before he could reply Beryl said, 'And there are things that I must speak to Mr Symthe about.'

Theodore said with a smile, 'Thanks for asking. Some other time perhaps?'

She nodded. 'Of course. And thanks again for a lovely afternoon.'

As she opened her front door she could hear Beryl's voice high-pitched and loud, followed by a peal of laughter. Her spirits that had risen so high during the afternoon now sank to their depths. She knew, without any doubt whatsoever, that Beryl resented the fact that she had been on an outing with Theodore and indeed resented her very presence in Kuwait. She wondered what the relationship was between her and Theodore; they were obviously very close. Far from welcoming Zena as one of the trilogy she seemed more likely to do her utmost to make it a twosome for herself and Theodore. Once again Zena saw the future as bleak and very, very lonely.

Then suddenly she remembered her reason for coming to Kuwait and decided to waste no more time before contacting Sami. She had a long and luxurious bath, then made herself an omelette. After having some fruit and coffee she went out to the hospital and dialled Sami's number.

CHAPTER SEVEN

AFTER some false alarms, when Zena looked eagerly out of the window only to see the cars she had heard driving on through the grounds, the most impressive of them all, a mink brown Rolls Royce slid to a halt outside her door. With a smile of happy anticipation she gave herself a final critical glance in the mirror to make sure that neither her eye-shadow nor lipstick was smudged. She was wearing her freshly laundered primrose cotton dress and her hair was caught at the nape of her neck with a slide from whence it fell to her shoulders in a sun-bleached wave.

When the bell rang she hurried to the door and opened it eagerly on someone who seemed to be an exotic stranger, in a cream *dishdasha* and headcloth which emphasised the darkness of his eyes and moustache.

'Why Sami, how different you look,' she cried, holding her arms out to him.

He imprisoned her hands in his. 'It is so good to see you, Zena.' His eyes, like black velvet caressed her so that she could almost feel the softness brushing her skin.

A shiver ran along her nerves and she turned her head away from his gaze. As she did so she saw, over his shoulder, a blaze of auburn hair like some fabulous flower as Beryl Bolitho made her determined way across the courtyard. She was not wearing uniform and Zena wondered where she was going with such obvious purpose. Her unspoken question was immediately answered as, with a knot of resentment, she saw Theodore walking to meet her. She dragged her eyes away and looked again at Sami. He had moved to the car and was opening the rear door for her. She took a step towards it then paused.

'Aren't you driving?'

'Why yes. Who else?' he asked.

'Then I'll sit in the front beside you.'

His eyes glinted and became unreadable. 'You will find it more comfortable in the back where the glass is tinted,' he said, waiting for her to get in.

'Oh that's all right, I'm getting used to the sun. I want to sit beside you.'

He hesitated a moment. Then he asked, 'Have you a scarf for your head?'

'Oh, you mean it is going to become hotter, I hadn't thought of that. Hang on a minute and I'll get something.'

She returned with a multi-coloured headsquare draped over her arm. She settled herself in the luxuriously upholstered seat and her feet sank into the deep-pile carpet. She exclaimed in wonderment at the numerous gold-plated buttons and switches on the dashboard. Sami was describing them to her, the two air-conditioning systems, telephone, television, stereoradio, heating, windows up and windows down contraptions, when suddenly glancing up she saw them again, Theodore and Beryl. Her heart beat a fierce little tattoo as Theodore eyed the impressive car with interest then casually glanced at the occupants. He turned to speak to Beryl then stiffened and came to a halt. He swung around and stared again, his gaze moving from her to Sami then back to her again. Before she could wave or make acknowledgment Sami had reversed the car and was racing it to the gates.

No doubt they were on their way to the harbour or bazaar. She was glad that Theodore had seen her with Sami so could not imagine that she was sitting alone waiting to be invited to make one of their party, especially as she would doubtless have waited in vain if Beryl had her way. She was happy to be with Sami, after all it was he whom she had travelled so far to see.

She looked across at his handsome profile. 'Were you pleased to get my telephone call and to know that I was here?'

His nostrils flared. 'It was fortunate that you rang before I had left,' he said sternly.

'Left? You mean you are going away?'

His voice held a tinge of rebuke. 'I told you, Zena, that if I did not hear from you soon I would return to England. Why did you leave it so long?'

'Oh Sami,' she said with a mocking smile, 'you don't like to be kept waiting, do you?'

'When exactly did you arrive?'

To her dismay Zena felt she could not tell him that she had been there for several weeks. She was guiltily aware that he would feel she should have got in touch with him before. She prevaricated by saying, 'Oh I . . . I've lost count of the days, everything is so new at the hospital, and I had to get settled in at the bungalow and . . . and the heat! I'm not accustomed to it, so when I am off duty all I feel I can do is rest.'

He took one olive hand from the steering wheel and laid it over hers. 'You will not remain at the hospital for long, my darling.'

Something tightened inside her, putting her once more on her guard. 'Well I have signed on for a year. It is good to see you, Sami. How have you been keeping? Have you had any more headaches?'

He forced his fingers between hers and a shiver ran down her spine. 'No, Sister Foster, I have had no more pain in my head; it has moved to my heart.'

'Dear me, Mr Gharbally,' she said with a laugh, 'I fear you have become a hypochondriac!'

It was a long drive from Kuwait through the straggling suburbs where architects had run riot with their designs for newly-rich oil workers, a hotch-potch of concrete houses reaching out into roads bordered by shabby faded advertisements, rusty abandoned oil drums and piles of bricks and rubble, waiting to be used for the many buildings that were in the course of construction.

'Do you live very far from Kuwait, Sami?'

'About an hour and a half from the town centre. It

doesn't seem as far now as it used to do because of the
suburbs that have encroached on the desert. It does not
look as nice as your country, would you say?'

Zena had to agree. The desert stretched pale and
unbroken save for the silvery pipe-lines than ran bearing
oil to the refineries and the ports. The sun seemed to be
just inches above her head and Zena was glad to put on
her scarf. Sami smiled his approval.

'That is better, but you would find a *mandeal* more
protection.'

'A *mandeal*? What is that?'

'It is what our women wear, a very thin dark scarf, not
so heavy as yours. I will buy you one, you will find it is
cool and comfortable.'

After a while Zena said, 'Do you realise that I don't
know the first thing about your family, Sami?'

'Isn't that why you are here? So that you may check up
that I am an honest man?' he asked, gazing straight
ahead.

She laughed uncertainly. 'You say you are one of
twelve children but how many are living at home?'

'You will soon see. There will be too many names for
you to remember just at first, but in time you will know
them all well.'

She said presently, 'Will they like me?'

'Of course. How could they not?'

'But your father . . . I am worried about him.' She
stole a glance at him.

His face tightened, his lips were momentarily compressed and she feared he was not going to reply, but at
last he said in a careful, explanatory tone of voice, 'My
father . . . is . . . he clings to the old ways, old customs;
he finds himself unable to move with the times. Nevertheless, he sends his sons to England to be educated,
although he must know that they might become westernised. It is difficult and would possibly have been better
for us all if we had not left Kuwait, for he cannot change
the way he is.'

'That is what I was meaning, Sami,' she said earnestly.

'I would hate to be the cause of disruption in your family.'

Sami looked in his mirror to make sure the road was deserted then drove off the highway. He turned off the engine, then reaching out for her he crushed her in his arms, his *dishdasha* enfolding her like a sheet, imprisoning her. When his mouth covered hers she returned his kisses but something was different from the previous occasion; she felt only the slightest emotional thrill. As if he was aware of her lack of response he released her and drew away.

'I . . . I'm sorry, it . . . it's this heat; I'm not used to it,' she said in an apologetic explanation.

His eyes looked deep into hers as he patted her hands. 'Do not worry, my darling. When we are married I will teach you to love me as much as I love you.' He turned on the ignition and drove back on to the road.

'Teach me?' Zena wrinkled her forehead. 'Surely love is not like that, Sami? You can teach someone to read or . . . ride a bicycle . . . but love is something you either feel or you don't. It is to do with the chemistry of the body.'

He shrugged her remark aside. 'You are speaking of the physical side of love and I know you love me in that way, I have had proof of that. Being a woman you will not on every occasion experience the same delight that a man does, but that is unimportant. It is the other side of love that matters.'

'But I still maintain that love of any kind cannot be taught,' Zena argued.

There was the tiniest pause then Sami said quietly, 'Here in our country we have happy marriages and united families, yet the man and woman have had little to do with each other before marriage; indeed they have never been alone together. But they know that their fathers who have their welfare at heart have chosen suitable partners for them and they know it is their duty to treat each other with the utmost respect and consideration. This leads to real love.'

Zena's eyes widened; she was surprised at his apparent change of heart. 'It sounds as if you agree with arranged marriages. Yet if you were to marry me you would be going against that; you would not be marrying the girl your father chose for you.'

His voice was as deep and soft as his eyes. 'That is because I have been fortunate enough to meet a girl that I love in every way. If it was just a physical attraction then I would not consider marrying her. But this girl fulfils each and every desire of my heart. She is kind and caring and very beautiful in appearance. I am speaking of course of you, my darling.'

Zena searched agitatedly in her mind for the details of their relationship, and all it amounted to was the gratitude that Sami felt for the comfort and companionship she had given him when he needed it, and the gratitude that she felt for the admiration and affection he had shown her. It was summed up in one word, gratitude.

'You know, Sami, that comfort and caring is an essential part of my work. To a certain extent I feel it for all of my patients, but that does not mean that I love them,' she said gently.

'Of course not and neither do they love you, they just appreciate you. But with me it is different because I do love you, and when I say that I will teach you to love me I mean that those qualities of yours, which have made me love you, I will return a hundredfold. I will show you so much kindness and caring that you will have to love me.'

Zena felt an apprehension in the pit of her stomach and her thoughts darted this way and that as she wondered what reply to make. She was able to break the increasingly long silence when she saw a plantation of trees.

'Oh look! I wonder why those trees are growning there in the middle of the desert?' she said, pointing towards them.

'That is made possible by distillation plants,' Sami replied, steering the car in that direction. Immediately an immense white marble building with a castellated parapet surrounded by a high wall, came into view. Zena laid her hand on his arm. 'Oh please stop, I must have a proper look at this. It's a palace, isn't it?'

There was a faint smile in his eyes. 'You like it, Zena? You think it is a little better than a mud hut?'

'It's super! Who lives there?'

'It is my father's house; I am glad that you like it.'

Zena chuckled. 'Pull the other one, Sami, it's got bells on,' she began, then bit off the words as he drove confidently through the large ornamental iron gates into an immaculate pink-tiled courtyard. Flowers and flowering bushes grew profusely on the roof and on the ground, and every one of the many window sills had its box of pink carnations. There were several fountains bordered by pomegranate trees which sprayed silver bright water into shallow pink basins.

Zena drew in a sharp breath. 'It is magnificent! Which part . . . I mean whereabouts does your father live? Is he the agent?'

Sami said simply, 'It is my father's house.'

Zena opened her mouth several times but could make no sound. When she could form the words she said, 'Then he must be a millionaire!'

He nodded gravely. 'That is so. Now we will visit him and you will please address him at first as Mr Gharbally and then as Abu Sami. In time you will get to know these things and become one of us for this will be your home.'

A delicious intoxicating excitement seeped through her body. This palace her home? Sami, the son of a millionaire, her husband? And she just a humble nurse at an English suburban hospital? It did not make sense; she must be dreaming. She shook her head and rubbed her eyes with her knuckles, then opened them half expecting the palace to have vanished, but it still stood there seeming, if possible, to look larger and more beautiful than before.

Sami parked the car beside a fleet of other cars of all makes and sizes, climbed out of his seat, walked around the bonnet and opened the door for Zena. She was untying the knot of her head square when he laid his hand firmly over hers. 'Keep that on, please,' he said.

Zena continued to loosen the knot. 'No, I don't want to do that, I don't need it, we are going indoors, aren't we?'

'I said keep it on,' he repeated sternly. 'My father will prefer that your head is covered.'

She met his gaze defiantly. Then the fight went out of her and she re-tied the knot. It really was a small matter, not worth arguing about. If it would help the situation with Sami's father it was the least she could do.

'Okay,' she said lightly, 'so I'm covering my crowning glory which seems to be my lot in life. As a nurse I've always had to wear a cap.'

He nodded briefly and ushered her through massive wooden doors, decorated with large iron bosses, to a marble-paved circular entrance hall with a wide majestic staircase which divided after a few stairs and led on both sides to the rooms above. He took her through an arcade of low arches and corridors, until they came to a large room two storeys high and divided into sections which were arranged around a tiled floor in the middle of which was a fountain of carved marble. Long couches uphol-stered in scarlet embroidered silk lined the walls, and the many low tables and stools were edged with ivory and inlaid with mother-of-pearl. Chinese porcelain and filig-ree silver-ware, incense burners and hookahs stood on pedestals in alcoves that had been built in the thickness of the walls. Elaborate chandeliers hung from the ceil-ing, and on the walls were embroidered inscriptions from the Koran, in crimson and gold and hung between panels of multi-coloured mosaic. Her eyes roamed the room, and she was so entranced by its luxury and beauty that she did not immediately see the man seated at the far end of the room.

When he came towards them she had no need to be told who he was for she could see that in the not so distant future Sami would closely resemble him. His dusky-skinned face was leaner, his nose thinner and more aristocratic. He had the same silky black moustache and thick hair, but also a beard, and his were faintly dusted with silver. There was an obstinate strength in the tight corners of his shapely mouth and a glittering determination in his deep-set eyes. He was a leader, the head of the household and he looked the part and was well aware of it. He briefly lowered his head in greeting.

'You are a welcome guest to my house and I am happy to meet you.' His piercing eyes took in every facet of her appearance.

'Thank you. I am glad to meet you, Mr Gharbally. What a magnificent house you have.'

The corners of his mouth relaxed in what could have been a smile. 'How is your health?'

'I am well thank you. And you?'

'My health is good, thanks be to Allah.' He indicated they should be seated and himself took a higher chair, and Zena wondered whether this was a deliberate manoeuvre so that they should have to look up to him. He was an impressive figure in a white *dishdasha*, his *kafiyah* bound with an *âgal* of gold and Zena had a vivid picture of him, riding across the desert on horseback with a protesting girl at his side.

He said with dignified politeness, 'I wish to thank you for the excellent care and the kindness you showed my son when he met with his unfortunate accident in England. Please believe me when I say I shall be eternally grateful.'

Zena gave an embarrassed laugh and shrugged a shoulder. 'Too much has been made of it; it is all part of the service and I did no more than any other nurse would have done. It would be nice if all our patients were as good and as grateful as Sami.'

A warmth came into his eyes as he slowly nodded his head. 'Gratitude, ah yes, I am glad that you realise his feelings are motivated by gratitude.'

He is warning me not to mistake them for love, Zena

thought. 'That is what I have told Sami,' she said.

The lines on his face visibly relaxed. 'And now that you have come to Kuwait I trust that you like my country?'

'You certainly have some most impressive buildings and the hospital where I work is excellently equipped; far better than the one I work in at home. But as for Kuwait itself I must admit I have seen very little of it so far.'

In the same conversational voice that he had used before he said, 'You have no husband?'

She felt herself stiffen in surprise. 'No, I have been fully occupied with my career; I haven't had much time to spare for romance.'

There was an expression of pride and arrogance on his face. 'I ensure that my daughters have a husband by the time they are fifteen.' He seemed so pleased with himself, so self-assured that Zena could not resist saying against her better judgment, 'Isn't that very young? It means they have no teenage life at all.'

His face became expressionless. 'Do you then consider that marriage is death?'

'No,' she said with an air of patient courtesy. 'Certainly not. But at fifteen a girl is still a child, there is so much to learn, to experience. Life is new.'

'And who better to teach her than her husband?' he asked, his eyes glittering.

'But surely she needs to learn about life before she has a husband or how can she be sure he is the right man for her? She has not had the opportunity of meeting others,' she protested.

He leaned forward, his face hard with challenge. 'Because he has been chosen for her by her wise and caring father. Can a child know better than a father who will make her the best husband?'

A feeling of frustation gripped her, tautening her nerves. She supposed she was being unpardonably ill-mannered in arguing with her host, but she pushed the thought aside. In all her life she had spoken out about the things she believed in and if she was to become a member of this household she must start as she meant to go on. Nevertheless her voice was a little subdued when she said, 'Yes I think she can. She is the one who has to live with the man, she is the one who knows whether he attracts her, whether she loves him. How can her father know all that?'

Mr Gharbally rose majestically to his feet, and with his unfathomable eyes and black beard and in his flowing robes he looked a most intimidating figure. Zena cringed inside as he said with deep disapproval, 'In your country many marriages are unhappy, and why? Because a girl may be attracted to some trivial thing, a man's hair-cut, the colour of his eyes, regardless of the suitability of his background and financial standing. But here, long, long before a daughter has reached puberty I make enquiries, research families, acquaint myself with characters, connections and prospects. Only then, after much thought and deliberation and prayer do I choose the man who is most suitable to make her a good husband. I do this because I care deeply for my family, for my sons as well as my daughters.' He let his dark, smouldering eyes rest for a moment on Sami.

Zena was impressed by his obvious sincerity as well as by the sense of his argument. I do believe he is right, she thought reluctantly. Maybe it is we who are wrong, perhaps that is why so many of our marriages end in divorce. There was still one point, however, that she felt the need to argue.

'But suppose your daughter does not like the man you have chosen for her? Has she no say at all in the matter?'

He raised his hooded lids in surprise. 'But of course she has. If she did not wish to marry the man I had chosen then she would not do so. I must make it clear that it is her happiness I am concerned with as well as her material welfare, and in turn my daughter would wish to make me happy by marrying the man of my choice.'

I give up, Zena thought resignedly. His motto seems

to be 'Heads I win, tails you lose.' We will never get anywhere by arguing.

'Your daughter is fortunate in having so caring a father,' she said courteously.

His face softened, the lines became ironed out. He said with disarming simplicity, 'My son is of more than marriageable age. I have chosen for him many wives without success, so far they have not pleased him. I wish him to be happy and have many sons, but that is in the hands of Allah.'

After they had spoken of other matters he said, 'You will take tea with my wife; she is expecting you. I hope you will visit us again. Now if you will excuse me I will bid you good-day.'

Once outside the room Zena felt a stab of uneasiness. 'I hope I didn't do wrong by arguing with your father, Sami? I'm afraid it was not very polite of me, but,' she shrugged her shoulders, 'that's the way I am.'

There was a pause, then he said, 'We prefer our women to be docile, Zena. I, having been educated in your country, am accustomed to hearing women give their point of view, but my father is not. Here it is the man who states his opinion and the woman who agrees.'

'The woman who agrees?' Her voice rose in an indignant crescendo. 'But if she doesn't? Isn't she allowed an opinion of her own? Is that how you feel, Sami? Wouldn't you like me to disagree with your views?'

He drew her behind a screen of potted flowers and clasped her to him. Then his mouth was hard on hers demanding response. When at last he raised his face it was to say, 'When you belong to me, when I have made you mine, you will not wish to argue with me or disagree with what I say because I will be your husband.'

'But . . .' Zena started to protest, but his mouth silenced hers with kisses and words, which although said in his own language were unmistakably of love. 'No more now, Zena, please. I will take you to the harem where my mother is waiting to receive you.'

Zena slewed around and pressed her feet firmly on the

tiled floor. 'The harem?' she repeated, her eyes wide
with dismay.

Sami's teeth gleamed white as he smiled at her. 'You
do not understand that word? The harem is the women's
quarters where you will meet my mother and sisters and
aunts.'

'And you will be there too?'

He raised his shoulders. 'I will not stay, I am not
interested in women's chit-chat. I will call back for you
when it is time to leave.'

The room where the women were was small by com-
parison with the other. The furniture was in reproduc-
tion Louis Quinze, dainty, fragile and decorated with
gilt. Women sat on chairs or on cushions, some were
wearing long, loose robes but the younger girls were in
smart, modern dresses. A television set was turned on
but the programme was disregarded by them all. Sami's
mother or Umm Sami as he said Zena should call her,
was surprisingly young looking to have had twelve children. She had a plump, unlined face, with a cloth on her
head held in place by a gold pin, and was dressed severely
in black. She greeted Zena with a charming smile and
enquired after her health. When she had been introduced to the other ladies they eyed her curiously, and
seemed eager to ask questions.

'Do you live in London?'

'In a London suburb,' she said.

'Is that Knightsbridge?'

'Oh no, but it is fairly near there. I go to Knightsbridge
when I have a day off from the hospital.'

'We go once or twice a year for our shopping,' Umm
Sami said. 'My husband books a suite for us at the
Dorchester hotel, and we all do our shopping in Har-
rods.'

'We also go to Paris, that is nice also. But how
fortunate you are to be able to shop in Knightsbridge all
the year round.'

Zena wanted to laugh. She would consider herself
immensely fortunate it she could shop there properly

just the once. Suddenly she caught her breath in her throat as she realised what being married to Sami would mean. She would be wealthy beyond her wildest dreams. She would be able to buy whatever she liked, wherever she liked and stay at a hotel which she had never imagined even entering. She could travel wherever she wanted in the car of her choice. What a far cry from her day in Knightsbridge with a toasted tea-cake and a slice of gateau as her treat. This magnificent palace would be her home!

When the subject of shopping was exhausted they questioned Zena on her health and way of life. Was there any reason why she had not yet married? On hearing that she was a nursing sister they told her enthusiastically the intimate details of their illnesses, their confinements and their children, so that Zena saw the wisdom of Sami placing himself elsewhere.

Her attention was drawn again and again to a beautiful young girl of about fifteen whom Umm Sami had introduced as Leila. Her hair was parted in the middle and hung to her waist in a black silk-like shawl, her eyes would have been beautiful had they not been so sad. She did not join in the conversation but sat on a cushion in a corner of the room, her small full mouth pouting. Zena asked her if she was still at school. She lowered her eyelids and whispered, 'Yes.'

'And have you been to England?'

She looked fleetingly at Zena and again said, 'Yes.'

A young woman dressed smartly in a flowered silk two-piece and wearing a great deal of gold jewellery on her neck and hands said to Zena in an aside, 'You must not mind Leila, she is very unhappy for the marriage which had been arranged for her may not come to pass.'

'What a pity. Why is that?' Zena asked.

'For many years it was arranged that she should marry her cousin and she is much in love with him. Now, however, he wishes to marry elsewhere.' She shrugged her elegant shoulders. 'She is a silly girl, she could also be his wife, we have told her that. But her cousin, he has said nothing as yet.'

They could not discuss it further for basins of rose-scented water were passed around for them to wash their hands and mouths. Tea was served, very sweet and milkless in small handle-less cups. Silver trays laden with sugary cakes were passed around, and Zena chose one which appeared to be of marzipan but tasted of spices she had not sampled before. It was so close-textured and cloying that one was more than enough. The conversation was beginning to be more than enough too. As a nurse Zena was accustomed to hearing talk about illness and symptoms, but these presumably healthy, well-fed women positively gloated over every facet of any real of imaginary discomfort that they or their friends had ever experienced; it seemed to be their greatest interest in life. Zena fought off an onrush of boredom and near hysteria, and it was with the utmost relief that she saw Sami arrive.

'Please come again soon,' Umm Sami said, and the invitation was taken up and repeated by all the other women.

As they were driving back to Kuwait Sami said, 'You like my father's home; do you also like his family?'

'Indeed I do, they were all so pleasant. What a beautiful girl Leila is, but so sad. Apparently the cousin she was hoping to marry is wanting to marry somebody else. Apart from the fact that she is, in my opinion, much too young to consider marriage, I should have thought the man would have welcomed her as a wife, especially as she seemed to be so much in love with him.'

Sami made no reply. Zena said, 'A lady I was talking to—I'm afraid I don't remember who she was—anyhow she said something very strange. She said that Leila was being silly to mope because she could also be the man's wife. What did she mean?'

Sami rested his soft, caressing eyes on her. 'She meant that according to the Koran a man is allowed to take four wives. Generally speaking the average man cannot afford to do that, but if he is wealthy enough to provide for them and all the children it is a good idea. Our country needs to be populated with Kuwaitis as I have told you.'

Zena was struck dumb by this piece of information, and a stab of uneasiness shot through her. When she was able she said, 'Then why is Leila sad? Doesn't she approve of that custom?'

When he made no reply she looked around at him questioningly and saw that his brows were drawn together and that his lips were tightly compressed.

'You ask too many questions, Zena. In any case the solution does not lie with Leila, it is for the man to make the decision. You would not understand, but there are other things to be taken into consideration. Now we will have no more talk of Leila, if you please.' His voice sounded final and commanding.

Later that night when she was alone in her bungalow and enjoying the comfort of a bath, it suddenly occurred to her that Leila was one of Sami's sisters. How frustrated then Abu Sami would be that his plans for both his daughter and son were being thwarted. Would he be willing for the beautiful Leila to become one of two wives? Zena remembered something that Sami had once said about his father, who already had twelve children, being still young enough to have more. Had he meant with another wife? Zena suddenly shivered although the bath water was still hot.

When she had dressed and was making a pot of tea there was a knock on the door. Her heart leapt. The only person likely to call on her was Theodore. She looked hastily in the mirror and shook her hair free from its slide. Small damp tendrils curled around her face which was pink from her bath. Her pulses quickened as she opened the door, but a uniformed Arab stood there. He handed her some parcels marked with the name of a boutique and the address of a well-known hotel. She took them indoors and opening the crisp white envelope that was with them extracted a gilt-edged card on which was written, 'Some small gifts, with my love, Sami.'

With a feeling of excited anticipation she opened the largest parcel first. She unfolded the layers of tissue paper and with an exclamation of delight lifted out the swathe of midnight blue chiffon and held it up. It was a long, loose kaftan-type dress exquisitely embroidered in cream and pure gold thread. Inside the neck was the label of a world-famous designer. The second box held the *mandeal* he had promised her, a long scarf in the same material. Eagerly she opened the smallest box and saw a pair of earrings fashioned in finest gold filigree. She clipped them on her ears and they were so light-weight she felt nothing at all. Then she draped the scarf around her head and held the dress against her and looked in the mirror. They were the most beautiful clothes she had ever seen.

Darling Sami! What marvellous taste he had and how generous he was! These were not birthday or Christmas presents but just gifts out of the blue, something she had never before received. She felt unusually feminine and pampered and basked in that state for a while. Then, gradually she had a smothered feeling in her chest. If she accepted these gifts was she committing herself irrevocably to the relationship? Did she want to do that? She still was not sure of her feelings. She loved Sami but did she want to marry him? Everything was more desirable than she could possibly have imagined, and yet . . . Here she was a foreigner who would have to adapt to a totally different way of life. But why shouldn't she? Why should she imagine that her own way was best? She was foolish to hesitate. Of course she wanted to marry Sami and she was extremely fortunate to have that opportunity.

That night she dreamed she was lost in the desert where arid tracts of beige land stretched as far as she could see. It was growing dark and she was lonely and terrified. Suddenly she saw the figure of a man on the horizon. As he drew nearer she saw with overwhelming relief that it was Theodore. He was wearing large dark glasses that almost covered his face. She ran towards him with outstretched arms but when she had nearly reached him he walked past her as if he hadn't seen her. He was so close that she reached out to touch him but there was nothing there. She turned and called his name, then saw that he was greeting Beryl. With their arms entwined they walked away leaving her standing alone.

When she woke in the morning her face was sticky with dried tears.

CHAPTER EIGHT

ZENA was checking supplies in the medicine room. Without an office of her own she felt unable to settle into the hospital routine or feel she was an important member of the staff. The position she held here was not clear and for the first time in her nursing career she sympathised with agency nurses who must feel as she now did, as if they were lending a hand to the regular staff without having any authority or status.

Beryl Bolitho, on the other hand, had somehow contrived to be in charge of everybody and everything. Her voice which was projected as if she was playing to an audience and had to be heard in the gallery, constantly echoed throughout the building from the sister's office which she had annexed for herself. She was clearly in her element. In no way had the unaccustomed heat drained her of energy; she positively glowed. Her red-gold hair had become even brighter and her movements brisker.

Zena, however, knew that she should never work here from choice. The atmosphere was the same as in any other hospital, there was the perpetual rattle of trolleys and clatter of dishes, the smell of bodies and food and air-fresheners, but there the similarity ended. She felt no genuine interest in the workings of the hospital, no involvement with the patients. So she found herself with more opportunity to browse over her personal problems. She was no nearer coming to a decision than she had been before she left Edgwarebury. She had uprooted herself from the hospital where she had enjoyed working and come all this way to find out more about Sami and his background. Now she had done that. She had seen him again and his palatial home which was beyond anything she had imagined. She knew that if she married him she would have everything she could desire including a devoted husband. But still for some unaccountable reason she was hesitating.

'Nurse, nurse.' The call alerted Zena from her reverie. There was the sound of hurrying footsteps in the corridor.

Walking swiftly to the door she almost collided with Nurse Karekjee. 'Oh Nurse Foster, please to come quickly,' she gasped, her eyes dark and tragic.

Zena wasted no time in questioning her but followed her to the ward where patients were agog with curiosity and standing around Mrs Patel's bedside. The woman was unconscious, her face the colour of putty, her hair damp with sweat, clung to her forehead. Zena turned to the chattering patients. 'Will you please get back to your beds immediately,' she ordered, then to Nurse Karekjee, 'Has she had her insulin injection this morning?'

'Yes, I know she had it at eight o'clock.'

'How long has she been like this?'

Nurse Karekjee hesitated. 'I—I am not sure, I was busy somewhere else.'

'Draw the screens and stay with her,' Zena said and hurried to the sister's room. With a mixture of relief and dismay she saw that it was Beryl who was on duty.

'Our diabetic is in a coma, Sister. She had her insulin and I would like you to confirm that she needs a sugar injection.'

Beryl rose to her feet immediately and with a swish of her skirt walked importantly to the ward, tossing questions to Zena over her shoulder.

'Did she eat all her breakfast?'

'I couldn't say, I wasn't working in that side of the ward.'

Beryl confirmed that a sugar injection should be given and when the patient regained consciousness told Nurse Karekjee to prepare some strong coffee to act as a stimulant. She turned to Zena. 'I would like a word with you in my office.'

A flush stained Zena's pale cheeks at the peremptory tone of her voice, which caused the patients to watch their exit with interest. They were scarcely inside the room when Beryl eyed her with freezing disapproval. 'Do you mean to tell me that no nurse in the ward checked to see that Mrs Patel had eaten her breakfast?'

'It would seem so,' Zena replied.

Beryl stared at her fixedly. 'A diabetic, admitted for special tests and treated with such inefficiency and down-right carelessness? It is unpardonable.'

'It was unfortunate, but luckily her condition was soon spotted so no harm has been done,' Zena said with exaggerated calm.

Beryl's round eyes became even rounder. 'Luckily? Luckily? In my ward patients do not survive by luck but through proper care and proper nursing. I am accustomed to having staff on whom I can depend otherwise I would very soon get shot of them, Nurse Foster.' Her tone of voice was a warning in itself.

'Sister Bolitho, I would like to remind you that I, too, am a qualified sister, accustomed to having my own ward. Yet you address me as nurse and treat me as one,' Zena said angrily.

Beryl studied her for a while without a word or change of expression. Then with an elaborate display of looking into the drawer of her desk she withdrew a paper. She read it through carefully then handed it to Zena.

'The vacancies that were filled by Mr Smythe were for one sister and one nurse. There was no question of two sisters being appointed.'

As Zena read the paper she had an odd sensation in the pit of her stomach. She shook her head perplexedly. 'I had no idea . . . I took it for granted that I would hold the same position here as I did at Edgwarebury, otherwise I would not have come here.'

Sister Bolitho stood by the door, her back rigid, her chin high. 'So you did not read the application form carefully enough. This must be quite a shock to you, but I trust your position has now been made clear. You may go.' She nodded a dismissal.

Zena knew that she had nobody but herself to blame

for this state of affairs. She had been over-eager to apply for the vacancy and more careless than she would have believed possible. Now, of course, Beryl's manner to her was understandable. At St Stephen's even more than at Edgwarebury the difference in status would be very marked. Beryl had no doubt resented her lack of deference as keenly as she had resented Beryl's air of authority. She knew how she herself felt about Sue. On duty she was very much the sister-in-charge and expected Sue to treat her as such, but off duty they were the closest of friends.

The patients were of various nationalities and either awaiting surgery with apprehension, or in a post-operative state, dependent on drips and drugs, or yet again mobile and ready to be discharged once their stitches had been removed. Before going to the theatre the patients lodged their valuables with the sister, who placed them in an envelope, sealed it and signed for it, then put it in the safe. When the patient was sufficiently recovered the items were returned to her.

Mrs Ussher from Los Angeles, whose husband ran a travel agency in Kuwait, had recently been operated on for the removal of her gall-bladder. Without her fashionable hair-do and pieces of jewellery she looked depressed and many years older. Zena decided that she would benefit from having these things restored to her.

'Would you like your hair done this morning, Mrs Ussher? The hairdresser has arrived and I think she may be able to fit you in,' Zena said.

'Thank the Lord!' she said, smoothing her hair with a quick, petulant gesture. As she brought her hands away she looked at them in disgust. 'And a manicure. It was only when they returned me my dentures that I began to feel at all human. Now if I can have my hair and personal appearance put right and get out of this ghastly garment maybe I will begin to feel half-way to being a female human.'

After arranging the appointment Zena took the en-

velope containing her jewellery from the safe, signed for
it and handed it to Nurse Levinson with instructions to
give it to Mrs Ussher when she had finished being
attended to by the hairdresser. 'Then pick out one of her
pink nighties and matching robe, because her husband is
coming to visit her later on and she will want to look her
best.'

Zena was free now to go to the canteen or to her
bungalow for a snack. She stood for a moment in the
courtyard in the blazing heat then decided to have
something in the canteen. She did not fancy a cooked
meal but there was always a good selection of fruit and
salads and drinks. She chose chilled fruit juice and bread
flaps with goat cheese. As she sat there she looked
around at the other nurses and doctors with a feeling of
emptiness, for there was nobody she knew well enough
to sit with and nothing to talk to them about if she did.
She had never felt more lonely. Then, brightening up the
whole canteen, she saw Theodore come in with two
other men. They were talking together, obviously discussing something of importance and had no eyes for
anything or anybody. Yet, just the fact that he was there
made the canteen seem a more friendly place and that
she was no longer alone any more.

The three men sat at a table and a waitress appeared
from nowhere to attend to them. There was no queuing
at the counter for them. Theodore lounged with one
elbow on the table and the other on the back of his chair.
He rested his square chin on his hand and looked at his
companions through his fringe of thick lashes. Suddenly
he threw back his head and laughed so that people
turned in his direction and smiled too at the happy,
infectious sound. Then his smile faded and he spoke
seriously and the other men listened and nodded in
agreement. Zena wondered what they were discussing
and why he was not lonely as she was. She watched until
they got up to leave then realised that it was more than
time she returned to her ward.

As soon as she reached it she knew that something was

wrong. Mrs Ussher's nasal voice twanged in complaint, Nurse Levinson's clipped English was all on one whimpering note and cutting across both was Beryl's commanding rasp.

I bet I know the trouble, Zena thought dryly; Mrs Ussher doesn't like the hair-style she's been given. Nothing else could cause such drama. She was sidling into the linen room to keep out of the way until whatever the trouble was had blown over when she heard her own name. 'And where is Nurse Foster?' Beryl asked.

Hastily picking up a pile of sheets Zena went nonchalantly into the ward and headed for a bed at the far end that needed changing.

'Nurse Foster, will you come here please,' Beryl ordered.

Zena joined her at Mrs Ussher's bedside and said diplomatically, 'Your hair looks nice; are you pleased with it?'

'Never mind my hair,' the woman snapped. 'Where are my earrings?' Her red-tipped fingers plucked petulantly at the quilt.

'Earrings? I don't know I'm sure. They would be where you put them.'

'They were put in an envelope . . .'

'Well I gave the envelope to Nurse Levinson to give you.'

'She gave me the envelope but not my earrings. Here is the list which was signed for, five rings, gold wristwatch, two necklaces, three bracelets, two pair of earrings. But one pair of earrings is missing,' she said bitterly, shaking the envelope to prove it was empty.

Zena turned to Nurse Levinson. 'Did you check the pieces over with Mrs Ussher when you returned them?'

The girl's eyes were huge and brown and tragic. 'No,' she faltered, shaking her head. 'You gave me the envelope and said to give to Mrs Ussher and I done that.'

'You did that, Nurse Foster? You mean to say that you did not tell Nurse that she must also check the contents?'

Zena's eyes flickered away from the cold and stormy expression on Beryl's face. She had taken it for granted that Nurse Levinson would go through the items with Mrs Ussher, but knew it was pointless to say so. 'I took the unopened envelope from the safe, gave it to Nurse Levinson and if she in turn gave it unopened to Mrs Ussher the contents must have been the same as when it was handed in,' she pointed out reasonably. 'Where is your jewellery now, Mrs Ussher? May I see?'

'Oh here you are,' the woman snapped irritably, taking a painted wooden casket from her bedside locker. 'But I'm not still anaesthetised, you know; I am quite capable of knowing whether it is all here or not. I can count two pairs of earrings.'

Zena tipped the contents on to the bed making certain that no piece was caught up in another but the earrings were definitely missing.

'What were they like?' she asked.

'They are gold filigree and my husband gave them to me just before my operation. Whoever has taken them needn't think they will get away with it. I didn't expect there to be thieves in the hospital or I would not have brought any jewellery in with me,' she ended nastily.

Beryl's bosom swelled and she seemed to grow an inch taller and more imposing. 'Now, Mrs Ussher, I warn you to be careful what you are saying. I will not have my staff labelled as thieves,' she said firmly.

'We'll see about that. Jewellery can't walk away by itself, or didn't you know? My husband will sue the hospital make no mistake about that. How will you like that?'

'Nurse Foster and Nurse Levinson, strip down this bed, turn the mattress, change the pillow-cases, clear out the locker and clothes cabinet, I want every inch searched. Those earrings must be found.' With a forbidding expression she stalked back to her office.

Someone had to tell Beryl that despite their careful searching there was no sign of the missing jewellery, so Zena decided to do that herself. She shook her head in reply to Beryl's raised eyebrows. 'No luck,' she said. 'I suppose it is certain there were two pairs?'

Beryl gave her a cold, penetrating stare. 'Indeed there were, Nurse Foster, for I signed for them myself.' She looked down at her desk as she said, 'Nurse Levinson mentioned that the envelope was not securely fastened when you gave it to her.'

'Wasn't it? Then perhaps they could have fallen out into the safe. I'll have a look.' Zena moved towards it but Beryl held up a detaining hand.

'Naturally I have already done that,' she said heavily. 'I am afraid that I will have to report this matter. I believe Mrs Ussher has every intention of lodging a complaint.'

'Well you can't really blame her I suppose. I wonder what can have happened to them?'

Beryl made no reply and Zena, mentally shrugging, returned to the ward where Mrs Ussher was still complaining bitterly to anyone who cared to listen, and shooting venomous glances in Zena's direction.

It was later in the afternoon that Zena was summoned to the office on the top floor. Instinctively she knew that it would be something to do with the wretched earrings although what they expected her to do about it she had no idea. Reluctantly she took the lift and walked along the thickly carpeted corridor until she came to the holy of holies and knocked tentatively on the door. A voice said, 'Come.'

When she entered the room her fears dropped away from her for it was Theodore who was seated behind the desk. She had not realised that he had been given an office of his own, but knowing him, she should have guessed. She was delighted to be able to talk this over with him rather than with a stranger. However, he continued reading and ignored her presence for what seemed a very long time. As she stood there waiting she saw that the sun had bleached his hair giving the brown a golden sheen. His hands were perfectly formed with long slim fingers, essential to a surgeon. He wore a beige cotton light-weight safari suit, and appeared what he was, an Englishman in a hot climate.

He looked up so suddenly that he caught her staring at him. She was dismayed to be vividly reminded of the first time she had seen him, when his attitude had been far from friendly. His eyes were clear and piercing, his mouth, drawn down at the corners, was stern. Nevertheless she smiled at him, but there was no response on his face.

'Nurse Foster, I have received complaints about you and I am very concerned. When I granted your application for the vacancy here it was because I wanted nursing staff from my own group of hospitals on whom I knew I could rely.'

'Complaints? About me? Why, what am I supposed to have done wrong?'

His brows drew together. 'It is not so much what you have done as what you have not done. There is the case of . . .' He looked down at a paper on his desk. 'Mrs Patel. I understand that you allowed her to go into a diabetic coma.'

Zena felt a rush of indignation. Surely there had been no need for Beryl to go rushing to Theodore about that incident.

'I didn't do the breakfasts on that side of the ward this morning. Mrs Patel and the nurses too, knew that she must eat everything she was given. I can't be expected to watch every patient while they swallow every mouthful.'

His eyes were angry and there was a snap in his voice as he said, 'Kindly address me as "sir". You are not here to argue your case but to listen to what I have to say and take note of it. As a member of my staff I expect you to be responsible for what the other nurses do, surely you realise that? Why else would I have brought you out here?' He lowered his eyes again and read something more then raised his long lashes to gaze at her shrewdly and steadily. 'About Mrs Ussher's earrings. What has happened to them?'

Zena shook her head. 'I have no idea, sir.'

'But you do know that the utmost care has to be taken of patients' property?'

'Of course.'

'The procedure is the same in every hospital. The items are accepted, listed and signed for and there should be the same system when they are returned. So what went wrong?'

'I . . . I just gave the envelope to Nurse Levinson and apparently she gave it to Mrs Ussher as it was. I was not there to see what happened then,' she said miserably.

He wrote something on the pad on his desk. 'Apparently Nurse Levinson says that the envelope was not well sealed down.'

'I didn't notice that when I gave it to her. She didn't mention it either.'

'But at some point the earrings have disappeared.' He frowned. 'That puts me in a very embarrassing position.'

'You, sir?' Zena's eyes flicked open wide.

'Of course,' he said tersely. 'I believe that the woman intends to sue the hospital—and why shouldn't she? She doesn't want to lose a piece of jewellery whether valuable or not. You signed for the envelope when you took it from the safe, so officially you are the last person who handled it. And I am responsible for you.'

'I am sorry, sir,' she said despondently.

There was a pause. Then he said, looking at her with remote grey eyes, 'This is most unfortunate, and if I have any further complaints about you I shall have to consider, very seriously, cancelling your contract and sending you back to England.'

Zena felt the humiliating colour flooding her cheeks, locking the breath in her throat. Before she was able to make any reply he said, without glancing at her, 'That is all. You may go.'

Once outside his room she fled along the corridor until she came to a bathroom. Only when she was behind the locked door did she allow a few tears to trickle down her cheeks. If she was sent back to England how could she ever face Miss Simms, Sue, any of the staff at Edwarebury or her own parents? Her career would virtually be at an end, for it would hold no chance of further promotion. Yet is was not that which caused her tears, it was the loss of the friendliness that had built up between her and Theodore. But what friendliness? That one pleasant afternoon they had spent together she had blown up in her mind out of all proportion. No doubt he had taken her out because he felt responsible for her recreation as well as her conduct. It had obviously meant nothing to him or he would not contemplate sending her away. She splashed cold water on her face and smoothed the hair around her cap. She was not going to give Beryl the satisfaction of seeing that she was upset.

Suddenly she knew that she could not continue to stay here fearing that any small lapse of hers would be relayed to Theodore by Beryl. One good thing had come out of this incident. It had made her come to a decision. She would accept Sami's proposal.

CHAPTER NINE

WHEN Zena replaced the telephone receiver she knew that once again she had shied away from committing herself. She had dialled Sami's number with every intention of telling him what she knew he was longing to hear, but had ended up by accepting an invitation to a party so that he could introduce her to more of his friends and relatives. It's better this way; I'll tell him afterwards, she decided, with an unaccountable feeling of reprieve.

She crossed the blistering hot courtyard to her bungalow and closed the front door on the rest of the world, thankfully. Without this opportunity for privacy, life here would have been insupportable. She showered and changed into a cinnamon brown dress which was only slightly darker than her tanned skin. She took the pins from her hair and brushed it free so that it swung to her shoulders in a pale gold cloud. She made some coffee and toast and picked up the book she was reading. After a while her own unhappy thoughts had been pushed aside and she was engrossed in the complicated whodun-it. The next potential victim was alone in a desolate house on a moor when she heard a shuffling sound and unexpected footsteps. At two-thirty in the morning! Then the sound of the doorbell set her heart thumping. Zena's beat frantically as well, for it had seemed so real. Then the ring came again and she knew that it was fact. With a shuddering sigh of vicarious panic she laid the book aside and went to the door.

Theodore stood there almost filling the doorway, blotting out the sunlight so that his face was in shadow, his usually light eyes like caverns. She faced him unsmilingly and in silence. He took a step forward and she retreated, then he strode past her into the room. 'Thank

you,' he said blandly, and Zena was so taken aback that
she wondered whether she had unintentionally and un-
wittingly invited him in.

'Ah, coffee, that smells good. Is there enough for
me?' He lifted the lid of the pot. 'Yes, I think there is.'

Zena automatically fetched a mug, with a strong wish
that she could have produced a plastic one for him.
'What did you want me for, sir?' she asked, her eyes
expressionless.

'There's no need to call me "sir" now, we are not on
duty,' he said, leaning comfortably back in an armchair
as if it was his by rights.

Zena perched stiffly on the edge of hers and waited
unsmilingly for him to continue.

'Well how do you like this place now that you have
been here longer? Have you settled down better?'

'I haven't seen any more of Kuwait since we went . . .
we went to the bazaar. As for the hospital . . .' she shook
her head so that her hair fell across her cheeks, 'I don't
like it at all.'

'You don't?' He looked faintly surprised. 'You liked
nursing in England and the work is the same. This
hospital is clean and modern; what don't you like about
it?'

She had a great longing to tell him all the things she
disliked. The fact that she had not been able to strike up
a relationship with the other nurses; her inability to
become involved with the patients; being demoted from
sister to nurse without being fore-warned, although that
was her own fault; Beryl, with whom she might have
expected to be friendly, being antagonistic towards her
and looking for misdeeds that she could pass on to
Theodore, and Theodore himself who had treated her in
so autocratic and unfriendly a manner. She thought of
his cruel threat to send her home in disgrace and knew
that the only thing she could mention was the loneliness.

He raised his eyebrows. 'Loneliness? Why, only the
other day I was about to call on you to see if you would
like to go to the harbour as I had earlier promised and I

saw you had another visitor.' He looked at her questioningly.

That would be the day Sami had called when she had seen Beryl and Theodore together. To have made a third with them would hardly have constituted a pleasant outing, she was sure. Thank goodness she had had another engagement!

'Did I?' she asked, her blue eyes wide.

He crossed his legs impatiently. 'You know perfectly well you did. And I must tell you that I was not at all pleased.'

The arrogance of the man! How dared he presume to be pleased or otherwise about her private life! 'That's too bad,' she said, and added softly, 'sir.'

'You are being silly,' he said casually. 'I want to know, if you have not been anywhere since I took you to the bazaar, where you met that Arab?'

'What on earth has that to do with you?' she asked furiously.

'Everything,' he told her blandly. 'While you are out here you are my responsibility. Tell me where you met him.'

'I will not,' she said defiantly, getting up from her chair to lean against the wall. Standing up she did not feel at such a disadvantage.

However he also rose to his feet and followed her across the room. He stood so close to her that she could see his blue shirt moving to and fro as he breathed. He placed a hand on either side of her on the wall, imprisoning her.

'You will tell me immediately or you will find yourself on the plane for England tomorrow.' His eyes, threatening her, were but inches from her own.

'I hate you, you're just a bully,' she said shakily.

'That is not what I asked you. I want to know where you met him.'

She looked frantically from side to side for means of escape, but watching her he moved even closer.

'If you must know he is a friend that I met in England.'

'In England?' He thought for a moment. 'He's not . . . hold on a minute . . . he's that chap who got shot in the head, isn't he?'

'You should know, you operated on him; you shouldn't have needed me to tell you who he was.'

'Why not? When I am working I look at the job I am doing, not at the anaesthetised face of the patient.' He dropped his hands and prowled around the room. 'How did you come to get in touch with him again?'

'I never lost touch with him,' she said curtly, infuriated at his catechism yet knowing she could do nothing about it.

He came back to her again. 'You are not telling me that you came out here hoping to see him, are you?'

'I'm not telling you anything. I'm having to answer your questions because . . . because you are bigger than I am,' she retorted.

The corners of his mouth twitched. After a moment he said, 'Right. I'll ask the questions. Did you come out here hoping to see him again?'

'Yes.'

'Why?'

'Why does anyone ever want to see someone again?'

He made a movement as if to take hold of her and she cowered away, scared by the ruthless expression on his face. 'He . . . he asked me to . . .'

'He asked you to come out here and you applied for that god-damned vacancy so that you could do so. Is that it?' he asked relentlessly.

'What is wrong with that? He is a very nice person.'

'A nice person? Nobody is questioning that. But what has that to do with you?' He gave her a long, curious stare.

'Or you?' she asked angrily. 'You may consider that you have the right to supervise what I do in the hospital, but you have no business whatsoever to dictate to me what I shall do in my private life. As to sending me back to England, you just try.' She swung away from him.

His hand shot out and spun her round to face him. She gave a gasp of pain as his fingers bit into her flesh.

'You don't believe that I could, do you?'

'I believe you would try to, but you wouldn't get very far. You see, Mr Gharbally . . . Sami . . . has asked me to marry him.' She raised her elfin chin and looked defiantly into his eyes. What she saw in them caused her heart to leap with fear.

'He what?' he thundered.

'I came here to see what the place was like before I gave him my answer.'

'What the place was like? To hell with the place. It isn't the place I am worried about; you can live where the devil you like. But not with him, Zena, you must see that.' The muscles around his mouth tightened.

'Well, I don't. He . . . he loves me and . . .' A flush crept into her cheeks as she continued, '. . . and I love him, and that is all that matters.'

He regarded with unblinking appraisal. 'No, that is not all that matters. Of course he loves you, you are beautiful . . . to some people . . . and you cared for him when he needed care. But you must not marry him. His ways, his customs are not yours. You are poles apart.'

She met his gaze candidly. 'But he is westernised. He went to school and university in England and has lived there for some years. He is no different from an Englishman.'

'Of course he is and will become more so. Even though he might think it would work, his family would never really accept you and that is for sure.' He spoke earnestly as he went on the prowl again.

Her eyes followed his movements triumphantly. 'Yes, they would. No doubt they would prefer him to marry a Kuwaiti girl but they love him and want him to be happy.'

'That is what he tells you,' he scoffed.

'I have met his family and his father told me that too.' Her eyes widened with admiration at the memory. 'He is a millionaire! They live in a magnificent house, like a palace, and they have a whole fleet of cars.' Her words died away as she saw the contempt in his eyes.

'So that is it! It's his oil-wealth that has turned your stupid little head! Can't you see further than his Mercedes or his Rolls, to imagine what life would really be like? Don't you know that in this country all women are considered inferior to men? That, generally speaking, they have to keep to their own quarters? How would you, with your colossal conceit like that?'

Zena collapsed on to the settee, her eyes wide in bewilderment. 'My conceit? What on earth are you talking about? I'm not conceited the least bit.'

He gave a snort of derision. 'The first time I saw you you thought you were monarch of all you surveyed in that hospital. It was "your" hospital, "your" ward, "your" staff, "your" patients . . .'

'Well, of course. I was . . .'

'When you gave an order you expected people to jump to it . . . including me, I do believe . . .'

'But I didn't know . . .'

'Maybe you didn't know who I was, but that's not the point. It was your attitude. I'll tell you something . . .' She made to interrupt him but he held up a warning finger, and continued, 'I thought it would do you the world of good to come out here and see what it felt like to be on the receiving end of that sort of treatment, to cut you down to size.' He eyed her, his head on one side. 'What would that be? Five foot three? Four? No matter. But you don't like it, do you? You don't like it one little bit.'

Her shoulders drooped and there was a hint of tears in her eyes. 'Oh, you are unbearable . . . and cruel. Of course I don't like being treated as if I am a junior when I know I am a darned good Sister. It wouldn't be natural if I did.'

Theodore threw himself on the settee beside her. 'You don't like being treated as an inferior at work, so how do you think you would like to be treated as an inferior in your everyday private life? To have to submit

to your husband in everything he says or does even
though it is very different from everything you have been
brought up to believe? To say goodbye forever to your
own country? To be classed as a foreigner? To be
without friends of your own? How would you like that,
Zena?'

She knew he was only repeating the problems she had
been trying to face, but she pushed that knowledge
aside. 'You are exaggerating everything. Actually, I can
well imagine some Englishmen thinking they were su-
perior to their wives,' she said, her eyes mocking him.

'Wives, that's another thing. Polygamy is still permitted over here. How would you like to be wife number
two or three or four?'

She turned aside from his penetrating gaze. 'I know it
is allowed according to the Koran, but is that so very
different from married men having mistresses, as they
frequently do in our country? At least polygamy legal-
ises everything and takes care of the wives and their
children.'

'Huh! That's another thing. How would you like to
have a child every year, which is considered the right
thing over here, and then when you were not fit to have
more, for your husband to take a younger wife?'

Zena rose to her feet and went impatiently to the
window. 'You are terribly biased and all you know is
what you have read somewhere. Do you always believe
everything you read in books?'

He slapped his forehead in despair. 'For God's sake,
Zena, so it may be exaggerated, but basically the differences between our ways of life are as I have told you. I
daresay he loves you and would want to treat you well
and have every intention of doing so, but his family
would never accept you as one of them. They consider
that English women have no morals, that they flaunt
themselves before men and make very poor house-
wives.' His voice was low and pleading and there was a
pleading look in his eyes. It was that look that made her
want to goad him.

'I shall be marrying him, not his family,' she said with finality.

He lunged to his feet and crossing over to her, stood towering above her, his hands on his hips, his thumbs in his pockets. His jaw was so squared that Zena eyed it as if it hypnotised her. 'Not if I can help it. Believe me, I shall do everything in my power to stop you. I wish I had had nothing to do with the wretched fellow's operation, that he had been taken to another hospital, and that neither of us had set eyes on him.'

'But we did, and I am grateful to you for saving him for me,' Zena said smoothly.

'B . . .' He spat the word over his shoulder and Zena flinched as if he had hit her. Then he swung around and sat on the edge of the table. 'Listen Zena, I am no racialist, believe me. I have met and worked with people of many nationalities and greatly admired a number of them, for their skill, their charm, their integrity. At times I have been physically attracted to the women, I admit. But I would never let it go further than that, for their sake quite as much as for my own. Do you honestly believe that this . . . crush . . . that you have for this chap would last for the rest of your life?'

'Crush?' Zena repeated wonderingly, for the word did not properly describe her feelings for Sami.

'For God's sake—' His anger soared. 'Call it what you like. I suppose you think of it as a grand passion. But will it last? Do you want to ruin his relationship with his family, muck up his life as well as your own?'

'Oh, no—no, of course I don't, you've got it all wrong. Sami says it will ruin his life if I don't marry him!' she whispered.

He prowled around the room again, half a dozen steps in each direction. His chin rested on his chest, his brows were drawn together. Suddenly he stood still and raising his head asked, 'What age is he?'

'He's—he's in his thirties—early thirties.' Then she added quickly, 'Old enough to know his own mind, you see.'

'He's also old enough to be married already. How do you know that he isn't?'

'He is about the same age as you. Are you married?' she flared.

He stared at her so furiously that she gave an involuntary shudder of fear.

'In this country fathers want their children to marry cousins to keep the wealth and property in the family. Why hasn't it happened with him? Has he got a cousin?'

'Yes, lots of them,' she admitted reluctantly. Then with a touch of sarcasm she added, 'Maybe he is married to one, two or three of them. That still entitles him to a fourth wife.'

'Oh my God! I was a fool to let you come out here.'

She drew herself up to her full height, her eyes flashed. 'Let me come out here? You are taking my welfare very much to heart all of a sudden. Maybe things would have been different if I had not been so lonely. You didn't think or care about that, did you? But Sami did. It is a great comfort to know that he loves me, that I matter to him,' she ended softly.

'Care? Of course I care. What the devil do you think I'm going on about if I don't care?' He glared at her irritably. 'Anyhow the reason I called here was to tell you to come along to my place this evening for a few drinks. I have some English and American visitors and I thought you would like to meet them. Who says I don't care?'

Zena felt drained of emotion. She would have liked to refuse his invitation which was more of an order, but the longing to meet and talk with people from England was too overwhelming.

'Thank you.' Her voice wobbled. 'What time shall I come?'

'Eight o'clock or thereabouts. Okay, I'll see myself out.'

When he had gone the room seemed empty. She sat on, her face buried in her hands, her mind a jumble of thoughts, her heart aching for Sami, herself and most surprising of all, for Theodore. How he would gloat if he knew that despite his nastiness, his cruelty, his dictatorial manner, he had wound himself around every part of her like a weed in an untended garden. Yes, like convolvulus, she thought bitterly, twisted around my heart and my thoughts and there is no way of getting rid of it. Or him. Whatever happened to her in the future she knew that she would always visualise him, with his bleached hair with the recalcitrant strand that persisted in falling over his forehead, so that she longed to smooth it away; his light grey eyes that stared at her with anger, contempt and something else—something that liquefied her bones and made her breath catch in her throat.

'I hate you, I hate you,' she muttered through clenched teeth. Then, unaccountably, she dissolved into tears, sobbing as though she would never stop. Why couldn't Theodore mind his own business? She had enough to contend with without his interference. It was not as if he really cared about her as a person; he would have reacted the same to any nurse who had gone to work on his staff. Then his offhand invitation to go along to his bungalow, never dreaming for a moment that she might refuse. And of course she hadn't. She knew that it would have been next to impossible for her to sit alone in her bungalow when she had the opportunity of being with him. Being with him? What was she saying! Being at his party was what she meant.

By half past seven Zena was preparing for the party with a measure of excitement. She wondered who Theodore's friends would be, and hoped quite desperately that there would be at least one woman with whom she could hold a conversation. If only Beryl had been friendly it would have made such a difference to her life out here, but she wasn't and Zena found it impossible to like her. She wondered yet again how Theodore could be so fond of her. Undoubtedly she was attractive and always well-groomed, and Zena had no doubt that she could be an entertaining and intelligent companion when she wanted to be, but with those people she did not want to impress she could be sneaky and unpleasant. Quite plainly she wanted Theodore to become a part of her life, and Zena believed that he was willing. She gave a wry smile. According to Theodore, in England women were considered the equal of men, but what would he have to say if she were to accost him and tell him that under no circumstances should he marry Beryl; that she was completely wrong for him? She knew without having to give it a second thought that he would be appalled at her audacity. And if he asked her to give a reason, what could she say? On the face of it Beryl was most suitable for him. They had trained together, worked together and both were highly thought of in the profession. If the particulars of each of them were fed into a marriage computer she believed they would be chosen for each other. The only surprising thing was that they had not already married one another. Beryl would be there tonight; that was a certainty.

She took out the long skirt and floral top that she wore to cheese and wine parties at home. She was zipping up the skirt when she stopped and stared at the blue kaftan that was hanging in the wardrobe. She took it out lovingly and held it against her, then with a smile of satisfaction she slipped it over her head. It reached the ground, covering her neck and arms and concealing her figure. Nevertheless, the graceful folds and the embroidery which shimmered and sparkled under the lights made her appear the quintessence of femininity. She brushed her pale gold hair into a pony-tail that fell from the top of her head to her shoulders in a thick, swirling wave; then she clipped on the gold earrings and wore no other jewellery. Her face, now honey-gold, needed little make-up; she merely accentuated the blue of her eyes with shadow and mascara, and touched her lips with geranium lip-stick. Once the sun went down the evenings became chilly but a coat seemed unnecessary for the short distance she would have to walk, so she carried the chiffon *mandeal*. All by courtesy of Sami, she thought with a pleased smile, and for good measure sprayed herself with some of the perfume that he had bought her in Knightsbridge.

The door to Theodore's bungalow was open when she arrived. Several men and women stood around but so far, to her immense joy, there seemed to be no sign of Beryl. Theodore was standing with his back to her, pouring drinks.

'Sandra, that's yours. And Jane . . .' He looked around for her and his words were cut off. He stood quite still, the glass in his hand, staring at Zena with rapt eyes as if he was seeing his first rainbow.

Feeling supremely self-confident at knowing she was looking her best she gave a friendly unselfconscious laugh. 'Did you think I was a W.P.C. come to arrest you for drinking alcohol?'

Surprisingly, the man, noted for his steady hands, spilled a little wine. 'No way,' he said, shaking his head very slowly.

He made the introductions. Most of the men were working as executives in the oil-fields, and their wives had joined them for varying periods. They were all so friendly that Zena, starved as she was of companionship, felt she wanted to hug and kiss them all.

'You're a cunning devil, Theo, first Beryl and then this gorgeous creature. I think I've got appendicitis coming on.'

'Have you got a spare bed for me, nurse?'

'I hope you take good care of her and don't allow her out on her own. She wouldn't be safe for a minute,' they joked.

'I keep a fatherly eye on you, don't I?' Theodore slipped his arm around her and was smiling teasingly down at her when Beryl made her entrance. She paused in the doorway, wearing a jade green trouser-suit, the colour a perfect foil for her hair. A cheer went up. 'Here she is, the lady of the lamp herself.' 'What lamp would that be? A red lamp?'

Beryl ignored their remarks and stared at Theodore and Zena. He released her immediately, and walking

ver to Beryl asked her what she was drinking. After
at first split second Beryl laughed and talked with
verybody and Zena could see why she would be popu-
r.

When there was a lull in the conversation she went
cross to where Zena was chatting with one of the
omen. 'Why, Zena,' she said, projecting her voice like
star performer delivering lines over a background of
urmurings, 'Those earrings you have on are very
retty. Gold filigree. They must be exactly like the ones
at our patient Mrs Ussher . . . lost.'

Zena felt the blood rush to her cheeks, causing her eyes
water, making her appear, she was well aware, guilty.
ne of the men who had been drinking steadily for a
ng time wagged a wandering finger in her direction.

'Been nicking an old lady's jewellery, nursie? Naugh-
, naughty.'

Theodore was suddenly by her side. 'These?' He
ouched the earrings with a gentle forefinger. 'They are a
ery popular design, you can get them anywhere. Where
id you buy them, Zena?'

She knew he was trying to protect her; she supposed
e considered it to be his duty as she was his responsibil-
y, and the knowledge made her feel physically sick. She
poke as loudly and clearly as Beryl had done. 'I have no
dea where they were bought, they were a present to me
om my fiancé.'

There was a friendly groan from the men present.
Her fiancé. Now she tells us!'

The change in the expression on Beryl's face was so
omplete that it could have been comical. She smiled at
Zena properly for the first time since she met her. 'Lucky
ou to have a fiancé with such good taste. They suit you
ell.'

Zena didn't want to look at Theodore; all she wanted
ow was to go home, but the guests were determinedly
iendly. When she felt she could reasonably leave one
f the women said she was having a few friends in on the
aturday, and invited her to come along.

'Saturday? I should like to come very much but have already promised to go somewhere else,' she said genuinely sorry that Sami's party would be the same day Theodore stared at her in disbelief and followed her from the bungalow.

'Goodnight and thank you for a pleasant evening,' she said, turning away. He followed her. 'I'll see you to your bungalow.' 'There is absolutely no need,' she said shivering in the cool night air and pausing to drape the *mandeal* around her head. He took no notice of her remark but strode beside her. 'You complain of loneliness but when you are invited to a party with one of my friends you refuse. Why? Didn't you like Elaine?'

'Yes I did very much indeed and I told her that I was disappointed that I couldn't go.'

'So where are you going?'

She sighed. 'To another party.'

'Whose party?'

'Sami's, if you must know,' she replied.

'And who is your fiancé, the bestower of gold ear rings?' His voice was sarcastic and ridiculed her.

'How dare you insinuate they were not given to me?' she cried, standing still and staring up at him in tormented fury. There was a disbelieving half-smile on his face to taunt her. Suddenly, goaded beyond endurance she raised her arm and struck him across the cheek, the slap sounding loud in the still of the night. Immediately she was horrified and caught her breath in dismay. He stared back at her for a moment with eyes that glittered with anger, then he tugged at her chiffon scarf pulling it away from her so roughly that her head was jerked backwards.

'Don't . . . please don't . . . you'll tear it,' she pleaded.

'I'll tear the damn thing to shreds if I see you wearing it again. Was that a present from the elusive fiancé too?'

'It was a present, yes. And my dress too. All of them presents from Sami, if you must know,' she said defiantly.

He hooked his fingers in the neck of the kaftan as if he would rip it off her. She put up her hands to protect it. 'Oh please,' she pleaded through trembling lips. 'Please don't tear this, it is the prettiest thing I have ever had.'

He slid his hands behind her back and drew her fiercely into his arms. Through the flimsy chiffon she could feel the strong beat of his heart, the firmness of his muscular body as he pressed her closer. Then his mouth descended on hers, kissing her as she had never been kissed in her life before. Her whole body seemed alight with a fire of emotion so that she burned with passions and desires she never knew she possessed. She felt his lips on her throat moving kiss by kiss to her ears and then her eyes. With one hand he loosened the knot of her hair and ran his fingers through it so that she shivered in ecstasy. Her lips searched for his again, eager to taste their sweetness. Suddenly he released her and pushed her away from him, so roughly that she stumbled and almost fell.

'So that is the way you behave behind your fiancé's back? You agree to marry one man yet eagerly fall into the arms of another? Isn't it time you came to your senses and stopped imagining yourself to be in love?' His voice was contemptuous.

Zena covered her face with her hands to hide her flaming cheeks. 'I . . . I don't think I have ever hated anyone as much as I hate you,' she said, her voice low and broken.

'No?' he asked indifferently. 'If your hatred is no more sincere than your love, then I have nothing to worry about, have I? Have you got your keys?'

He unlocked the door and pushed her gently inside. 'Now you can have a little weep and a good night's sleep, and you will feel fine in the morning,' he said casually.

Furiously she slammed the door shut on him, then did just what he advised. She sank down on the nearest chair in a soft blue heap with her golden hair running riot and tears of anger and disappointment streaming down her cheeks.

CHAPTER TEN

It was yet another hot and humid day and as Zena looked up at the relentless white sky she yearned for the sweet freshness of rain on her face, and the softness of wet air; the kind of weather she deplored when she had more than enough of it in England.

When she reached the ward she was alert for the sound of Beryl's resonant voice, and wondered what carping criticisms she would have to endure today. Surprisingly there was no sign of her when she passed her office, but soon after Zena arrived in the ward Nurse Levinson sidled up to her like a sleek black cat.

'Sister Bolitho will not come today,' she said, her dark eyes enormous.

Zena was ashamed of her feeling of relief. 'Did she say why?'

Nurse Levinson giggled, a tinkling sound. 'She say she have a tommy-bog. Is that right, please?'

'Yes, that's quite right. A virus or something she has eaten or drunk has upset her stomach and given her pain, possibly made her vomit,' Zena explained with suitable actions.

The nurse nodded agreement. 'Yes, I think so. A tommy-bog,' she said happily.

With new zest now that she was temporarily in charge, Zena did her ward round, questioning the patients as to their comfort and symptoms, reading their charts and collecting them for the doctor to see. Mrs Ussher was sitting beside her bed looking like a night-club queen in be-ribboned nightdress and matching negligee, with lacquered hair, heavy make-up and laden with jewellery.

Now for the complaints about her wretched earrings all over again, Zena thought as she approached her

'Good morning, Mrs Ussher, you are looking very smart; you should be in a fashion parade,' she said amiably.

The woman raised heavy lashes. 'That's what my husband says. "Darlene," he says, "I am a very, very fortunate man that I have such a very attractive wife. I don't mind what money you spend, you are worth every dollar." In my opinion it is just laziness on the part of these women who drool around looking a mess. They don't deserve to keep their husbands, yet they are the first to complain when they go after someone more attractive,' she said complacently.

'Perhaps they haven't got such a wealthy and generous husband as you have, Mrs Ussher; you are very fortunate. Not so lucky with your earrings, though. I wonder what can have happened to them?' As soon as Zena had said the words she was furious with herself for mentioning them and starting up the subject all over again.

Mrs Ussher touched the lobe of an ear with a red-tipped fingernail. 'Here they are.'

Zena stared at the gold filigree earrings which were so like her own but somewhat larger and more ornate. What happened? When did they turn up?'

She laughed airily. 'I was wearing them all the time. I remembered afterwards that I put them on as soon as the hairdresser had set my hair. None of you silly nurses thought to look at me, did you?'

Zena gave an exclamation of annoyance. 'Really, Mrs Ussher, I do wish you had told us, it would have saved us a lot of worry. We don't like patients' things to be mislaid.' Of all the irritating women! All that to-do when she thought she had lost them, all the trouble it had created with Theodore by the threat of action being taken against the hospital and then to casually discover that she had them all the time and not be bothered to tell anyone.

'But I did! I told Sister Bolitho straight away. Didn't she tell you?'

Zena shook her head. 'She probably didn't see me again,' she lied.

So Beryl had known even before she reported the los
to Theodore. Or rather, the non-loss. She had known
too, when she made that defamatory remark at th
party. Without any doubt she was determined to discre
dit Zena, especially in Theodore's eyes. Well, two coul
play at the game. She would go to Theodore's offic
when he had finished his out-patients' clinic, and let hin
know just what sort of a woman Beryl was; show hin
that he was not so clever at judging character as h
thought he was. But even as the hasty thought formed i
her mind she knew that she could not do it; he must fin
out for himself. Moreover she knew she could not fac
him so soon after last night, the memory of the closenes
of his body, the feel of his arms around her, his lips o
hers was still too vivid, too breath-taking. What she mus
now do was to put him completely out of her mind
Tonight was Sami's party, and then she would stop al
this shilly-shallying, agree to marry him and insist tha
the marriage took place as soon as possible.

Somewhat to her surprise Sami did not come for he
himself but at seven-thirty a chauffeur-driven car ar
rived. Wearing the beautiful kaftan seemed somethin
of an anti-climax after last night when it had been s
thrillingly new. She examined it carefully to make cer
tain there was no tear in it from Theodore's angr
fingers. At the thought of them the blood course
through her veins, and as she tended her hair her scal
tingled with the memory of his touch. Suddenly over
come with emotion she flung herself on to her bed an
beat the pillows with her fists. 'Blast him! Blast him
Why can't I stop thinking about him?' she groane
through clenched jaws.

When the large silver grey limousine arrived and th
chauffeur rang her bell she draped the *mandeal* over he
head and stood outside her bungalow for a full minute
pretending to check the contents of her handbag befor
getting into the car, in the hope that Theodore might se
her and realise that she did not give a fig for his orders

But on the dreary journey her mind returned to Theodore's warnings. He must be wrong in saying that Sami's family would consider that western women behaved indiscreetly and had no housewifely skills, and would disapprove of a wife who had not been chosen by his father, or why would they be holding this party for her? Yet what hell it would be if he just happened to be right! Imagine living with the kind of disapproval and fault-finding she was experiencing from Beryl, not just during working hours but every hour of every day. Such disapproval would be bad enough if she lived with Sami in a house of their own, but how intolerable to be in Abu Sami's household.

The fact that women were considered inferior to men and that wives had to obey their husbands in everything was against all her instincts, although she had to admit that the craze for equality for women had not done a thing to ensure happy marriages; rather the reverse. Polygamy? She tossed that possibility aside. Sami was too westernised, too fond of her to indulge in that. Children? To have a number of them looking like Sami would be marvellous. But as she tried fondly to picture them they all had light brown hair, pale skin and clear grey eyes. She moved restlessly on the luxuriously up-holstered seat; she had no right to think that way, for whether she married Sami or not, one thing was certain, she would never have Theodore's children. But with that knowledge her heart felt desolate.

She stared blankly ahead, mulling over what he had said. Then she pushed the thoughts aside and set herself to thinking of the good things that she would enjoy, things that Theodore had omitted to mention. No longer would a day in Knightsbridge be a special treat. When she was in England on a shopping spree she would buy all her things there and have them delivered to their suite at the Dorchester. Then, maybe, she would decide to spend a few days in Paris. There would always be a choice of cars at her disposal and the palace with all its luxury would be her home. She gave a guilty start. How mercenary she had become! She should be thinking about her life with Sami, and her feelings for him.

How did she feel? When he kissed her she felt an immediate response, for it was a new and wonderful experience for her to be loved. And he did love her she was certain of that. He had every virtue; he was grateful, generous and caring, and he was handsome too. She smiled to herself as she thought 'he is rich, dark and handsome, which is what every girl is supposed to want in her lover, so who am I to look for something more?'

The house was flood-lit and gleamed white like a fairy-tale palace. The wide beam of light shining on the banks of flowers on the roof and in the courtyard enhanced their colours and made them appear artificially bright. From the fountains the water sprayed like finest liquid gold.

As Sami greeted her she was dismayed to see shadows like bruises beneath his eyes, and that his skin appeared to be unhealthily colourless. He held out his arms to her. 'My darling, you look even more beautiful than I had pictured in the dress I chose for you. I hope that you like it?'

Zena looked down at it fondly. 'I love it, Sami. You are so kind and have wonderful taste. It is the prettiest dress I have ever seen. How clever of you to know what to buy.'

He smiled indulgently. 'No Zena, not clever. You would look perfect in anything. I merely chose what I liked myself.'

Abu Sami greeted her hospitably, allaying any doubts she had of his approval of her. He looked swarthier than she remembered, his beard and moustache seemed thicker and blacker. His eyes were not gentle, as Sami's were, but jet black and piercing. She was introduced to a number of men of similar appearance who eyed her calculatingly, whether in a friendly spirit or not she had no means of knowing.

The party was held in the huge reception room, two storeys high, with a fountain playing in the centre.

Against the walls guests were seated on couches or firm oblong cushions. Around the room gilded pillars supported an ornamented frieze sculptured in plaster decorated with gold. On the walls hung priceless Oriental carpets and similar ones lay on the floor. In a lobby that adjoined the room the guests had left their shoes, and Sami waited while Zena removed hers. The women wore a great deal of heavy make-up, expensive smelling perfumes and a vast amount of gold jewellery set with diamonds. Their clothes, either long skirts or silk trousers with hip length tunics were in a variety of rich colours. Zena's eyes were drawn almost immediately to Leila, looking so young with her rounded cheeks and still slim body, who was seated cross-legged on a cushion in the corner of the room. In a turquoise trouser suit she looked like a pretty flower.

Zena looked around for her hostess but Sami told her that his mother sent her apologies and welcomed her. 'My mother is of the older generation and she and some of her sisters do not join a party when men are present. They prefer not to.'

'Then shall we go and speak to your sister?'

'But certainly. Nawara is over here and Fatimah . . .' He moved towards two plump young women who were lavishly dressed and heavily be-jewelled.

Zena caught at his arm. 'I meant Leila, she looks so lonely.'

His eyes as he looked at Zena were unfathomable. 'Leila is not my sister. What made you think that she was?'

Zena turned to him in surprise. 'I—I don't know exactly. I just imagined that she was.'

'No. Leila is my cousin. Her mother is my mother's sister.'

With a sudden shock realisation flooded over Zena. 'Your cousin? Then . . . then is it Leila whom your father wished you to marry?'

Sami nodded his head. 'That was the intention. Until I met you and fell in love.'

Zena's eyes grew dark with pity. 'But she is very much in love with you, Sami. Before you met me . . . did you think that you loved her? Did you ever tell her so?'

'You must not ask these questions, Zena. We do not speak of such things,' he said shortly, irritation in his voice. His eyes were suddenly as piercing as his father's, his mouth as relentless.

Zena's body stiffened. 'I must speak of them, Sami; I have a right to know. Have you told her that you loved her?' she persisted, disregarding his obvious displeasure.

He covered his face with his hands and smothered a groan. 'No, no, I have never done so. Indeed I have never spoken to her alone,' he said wearily.

'You haven't? Then how can she possibly know that she loves you?'

'I have explained this to you before. It is because she has been brought up expecting to marry me. So for many years she has been loving me in her mind so that when the day of the marriage came she would make me a good wife. Now I forbid you to talk of this any more.'

He was moving away but Zena laid her hand on his arm. 'Just one more question, Sami. When the lady I spoke to the other day said Leila could marry the man she loved and become his second wife, was she meaning her . . . and me?' She had a hollow feeling in her chest.

Sami appeared to be trying to find the right words. When at last he spoke it was in a cool, distant voice. 'She was, yes, but she did not know the circumstances. As I told you, polygamy, in this case, was out of the question.'

She ran her tongue across her lips. 'Because . . . because I am English?'

He frowned. 'No of course not, that would make no difference if you were my wife.'

'Then why?' Her voice was husky.

He leaned against the wall, gripping the edge of a carpet that hung there. 'Because it says in the Koran "If you fear that you cannot love equally then marry only one . . . do not love one to distraction to the prejudice of another whom you keep in suspense." And as you know, darling, it is you I love to distraction. So how could I take two wives? It would be against my religion.'

Zena moved closer to him. 'Oh Sami, I know you love me now, but that sort of love cannot last, not with the same intensity. It is bound to die down, to change, become more a way of life. What then, Sami? What would happen then? Would you take another wife?'

He closed his eyes and looked unutterably weary so that she felt resentful towards Abu Sami, whom she believed had been putting pressure on Sami to change his mind and carry out his father's wishes with regard to his marriage. She felt unkind in continuing with her questions but knew they were fundamental to the happiness of both of them. She needed to have the answers.

'You must meet my guests, Zena. They will be thinking I am ill-mannered not introducing to them my beautiful wife-to-be. Come now.' He made to urge her forward, but she drew back.

'No Sami, not yet; they can wait a little longer. You have not answered my question.'

He ran a hand over his face. 'You ask hypothetical questions. You disobey me . . . maybe I would do better with a wife who knows her place.' He smiled gently so that she did not know whether he was being serious or not.

Almost as if he was here beside her she seemed to hear Theodore's warnings, so she waited for Sami's answer, determinedly.

He ran his fingers through his hair and sighed. 'How can I answer you when it is impossible for me to believe I will not always love you as I do now? You are a silly girl to worry over such non-events. If you were marrying an Englishman, would you ask him if he would later take a mistress? Would you expect to get a true reply?'

'What I really want to know, Sami, is if you agree with the principle of a man having several wives.'

He smiled down at her, his eyes soft with love. 'I can imagine that sometimes it would be a good thing. Indeed I have heard it said that a wife is often happy and relieved when her husband takes a younger wife on whom he lavishes his attentions. And in my opinion that is far more honourable than for him to take a mistress, as happens frequently in your country. And now, my darling, I positively refuse to answer any more of your foolish questions.'

When she had met all the relations she knew that she liked them but equally she knew she could never remember all their names. Bare-footed Arab boys wearing white suits brought coloured water and towels for their hands, followed by trays of sumptuous foodstuff sufficient for a banquet. When they had finished eating ewers were again brought in and braziers of incense sweetened the air.

Zena noticed that the men and women had automatically separated, and sat at the opposite ends of the room, and the food had been passed to the men first. They talked and laughed loudly amongst themselves, speaking in Arabic, while the women chattered endlessly of their health and families. It was of no interest to Zena, and she looked down the room at Sami wishing she could be alone with him. He was the centre of a group of men and she was concerned to see the exhaustion on his face. She glanced at Leila in time to see her give a sudden shy peep at Sami through her lashes. Everything about her seemed to be sad, the angle of her head, the droop of her shoulders, her gently pouting mouth and Zena felt a wave of fierce maternal affection for her. Poor little girl, caring so much for a man she did not really know.

As she looked around the room the feeling gradually crept over her that she had no right to be here. She did not belong, nor would she ever belong in these affluent surroundings where everything was so different from what she was accustomed to. She looked from her bare feet to the group of black-eyed men in their flowing robes and head cloths, and over to the women, and had a sudden frantic longing to get away. It would be wrong from every point of view for her to marry Sami even though he was at the moment in love with her; she could only cause disruption in his family. Leila, the girl chosen by Abu Sami, was the one who should be his wife and one day Sami would surely be grateful to her for realising that this was so.

As for her own feelings, she cared for him deeply and had been sufficiently attracted to him to come out here to see him in his own country. He had been kind, and nothing he had done was responsible for her decision, neither were the customs of his country entirely to blame. The real reason, incredible though it seemed, was that self-opinionated man who seemed actively to dislike her and was plainly attracted to Beryl Bolitho, Mr Theodore Smythe. For how could you marry one man when another cast a spell over you so that when you were awake you thought constantly of him and his warnings, and when you were asleep you felt the night was wasted unless you dreamed of him? His firm long-fingered hands, his unruly brown hair, his clear grey eyes, his voice, even the angry words he had spoken had so infiltrated into her being that if, before she had known him, she had been a thread of silk, now that thread was a part of a patterned fabric. She might not like the design but she was in it for all time and nothing, neither cutting nor tearing could separate her from it.

Her heart ached at the thought of telling Sami her decision, and she would have done much to have escaped the necessity, but the sooner she told him the better. She excused herself to the women, and their chattering stopped as she walked the length of the room to where Sami was talking with the men. They too fell silent as she told Sami it was time she was leaving as she had a long journey.

He nodded agreement and went to place his cup on the table but instead it fell to the floor. Once outside the room Zena said, 'I must speak to you alone, Sami; we have had so little opportunity.'

'Not more questions,' he pleaded, but led her to a small open-fronted room nearby.

'Darling, I dare not be alone with you for long, it would not be proper. You know how much I want to hold you close, to feel the softness of your beautiful hair and the warmth of your lips but I must wait until you are really mine and I am becoming impatient.'

Her heart beat rapidly. 'That is what I want to speak to you about,' she said breathlessly.

'My darling, I am so glad you have decided.' He drew her close and fastened his mouth gently on hers. She loved the feel of his arms around her, the pressure of his lips, and as his hands moved down her back she gave a shiver of pleasure and moved closer. Then she placed her hands on his chest and pushed him away for she knew she was not being fair to either of them.

Sami looked at her with pain in his eyes. 'What is the matter? Why do you draw away from me?'

Her heart seemed to contract as she looked at him. 'Sami darling,' she said gently, 'I am very, very sorry, but I cannot marry you.'

He looked puzzled as if he had not heard her correctly. 'What are you saying, Zena? I don't understand. You love me, I know you do. And I love you so very much.' He held one of her hands in both of his.

'I know that you do, Sami. And it is true that I love you too. But I can see that it would not be right to marry you.'

'Not right for two people in love to marry? You can't mean that,' he said hoarsely.

'I do, Sami. Your father is right in his choice of a wife for you. He knows that Leila would be willing to put you first in everything, and I could never do that. I have not been brought up in that way. I like my career, I like my independence and I like the company of men as well as women. I could never conform to your customs. Besides, I love my own country as you do yours; it is natural.'

He closed his eyes as if he was in pain. 'These are all

things that can be resolved. Our love would make such differences unimportant. We could live in England at first, if you wanted, then you could follow your own customs. But I do not believe you would want to do that for long. Some of my sisters and cousins who have been to your country were happy at first to have their freedom, to wear western clothes and talk with men, but now they do not want it any more. Of their own choice they have returned to our traditional way of life because they realise that is the way of happiness. You love me so why should you want to talk and mix with other men?'

She knew that they could never agree over this. She could not argue for he would use all his persuasive powers to win her over, try to prove to her that she was wrong.

'Because I do not love you enough, not in the way you want me to,' she said firmly.

He stared at her as if he was not really seeing her, then he closed his eyes, shook his head and looked at her again. 'You cannot mean this, Zena. To me you are my mother, my friend, my child, my wife. Don't rob me of them all,' he pleaded.

She felt tears pricking her eyelids and had to fight the desire to take him in her arms and comfort him. She bit her lip until her teeth sank into the flesh, knowing that if she weakened now it would be the end of her struggle.

'I am sorry, Sami, so very sorry, but, as I have found in my nursing experience, sometimes you have to be cruel to be kind. It hurts to have something cut away but sometimes it is necessary and would do far more damage to leave it. I know I would be wronging you if I married you and I love you too much to ruin your life . . . to ruin both of our lives. Will you accept what I say and let me go?' She lowered her eyes and prayed that tears would not fall.

She felt his arms come around her again and he drew her gently against him. Then his cheek rested on her golden hair and he murmured words that meant love in any language. He cupped her pale, heart-shaped face in his hands and placed his mouth on hers for what seemed an eternity. At last his hands fell to his sides and he turned sadly away.

'You will please forgive me that I will not accompany you home. I could not bear to be with you knowing that every minute was taking us nearer to the parting. I will have the car brought for you with my very best driver. I cannot say goodbye.' His voice broke.

With her head downcast she fought with her emotions, striving not to break down, and when at last she was able to look up he had gone.

CHAPTER ELEVEN

ALL night long Zena lay sleepless. The fact that she had at last told Sami of her decision did not bring her the ease of mind that she had imagined it would. She could not forget the sorrow on his face, could not bear to think that she would never see him again, never hear his gentle, loving voice. It was like losing a son, she imagined, for he was someone she wanted to hold in her arms and protect from any unpleasantness, feelings which had been awakened when she tended him in hospital. She knew that she would find it intolerable to remain in Kuwait when he was just a phone call or a short drive away. She would have to return to England and find work of some kind until her year's leave was up, but at that thought she was filled with bleak despair, for, in all possibility, that would mean she would not see Theodore again either. It was a relief when morning came, and as it was a major operations day she knew she would have no time to dwell on her own problems.

Beryl was still on sick leave and there was a general shortage of staff. Four patients were going down to theatre from Zena's ward and she checked that they were prepared. Mrs Ussher, looking very glamorous, was being discharged later in the day. An elderly patient accidentally upset her fruit juice and Zena went to the linen room for fresh bed-linen, feeling thankful that disposable sheets and pillow-cases were used here. As she was stripping the bed the telephone rang in the sister's office. Calling to Nurse Shah to finish off for her she hurried to answer it. It proved to be a call from Casualty informing her that a patient had been admitted and was to receive immediate surgery. Sister Bolitho was required to be in attendance.

'I'm sorry, she is still away sick,' Zena said, about to replace the receiver.

The voice sounded harassed. 'So she isn't back yet and we've got three others of the staff away. Can you send us her deputy? It is urgent.'

Zena weighed up the situation in her ward. There was no patient whom she was unduly worried about and it would be several hours before the post-operative patients would need attention, and the nurses on duty should be able to cope.

'Yes, I will come myself. It is Sis—Nurse Foster. Which theatre will be used?'

'Theatre five and thank you. As soon as you can, please.'

Zena had done her share of theatre work at Edgwarebury, and, although she had not cared for it, at least she knew the procedure. She made a hasty round of the ward and gave Nurse Shah some instructions.

'I don't know how long I will be gone but will you please stay on duty until I get back. Nurse Levinson will be here in a few minutes.'

She took the lift to the ground floor and walked along the dim corridors towards the Casualty department, glad of the change of work. She pushed open the door and saw the usual number of patients waiting for attention, chiefly road accident victims with broken limbs and lacerations. She reported to the enquiry desk and was directed to a cubicle at the far end of the room. A patient was lying on a high bed, his eyes closed as a nurse asked him questions and filled in a form with his answers. Zena stopped dead on the threshold and her hands flew to her mouth as if to stop herself from calling out, for it was Sami who was lying there in need of urgent surgery.

For a moment compassion fought with reason, she wanted to go to him but knew she must not cause him emotional stress. Controlling her desire to speak to him she hurried from the cubicle to the theatre. Undoubtedly Theodore would be performing the operation as Sami had been his patient. She put on a gown and mask and switched on the lights. She laid out gloves and dressings and then the instruments. She filled the sterilizers with bowls and dishes and had just checked that everything was ready when Sami was wheeled in. A doctor and nurse lifted his unconscious body on to the table, then went to scrub up. Then Theodore arrived and looked carefully around the theatre checking that everything was to his satisfaction. Then he studied the X-ray films. After a few moments he went over to Sami and listened to his chest and took his pulse. His hands moved gently over his head then he nodded in Zena's direction.

'Cut away the hair, please, in this section.'

As she touched Sami's silky hair she gave a long, quivering sigh and her hands shook. Theodore swung around immediately to look at her. Then he looked again with recognition.

'Nurse.' He called her aside. 'Please leave this theatre immediately and send in a replacement,' he said authoritatively.

'There is nobody suitable who is available, sir, several of the staff are away sick and the other theatres have full lists.'

'Then exchange with a nurse from another theatre.' His eyes seemed to bore into hers. 'You must realise that you are too involved.'

Zena felt she must stay, that her presence would in some way help Sami. 'I will be all right, sir. In here he is just another patient.'

'It is a tricky operation . . . are you used to theatre work?'

'I have done my share and . . . and I should very much like to assist if I may,' she pleaded, her eyes raised to his.

He hesitated a moment, then gave a brief nod. 'Very well. Carry on.'

After he had scrubbed up, a junior nurse tied him into his gown. Zena completed her task, leaving a bald area on Sami's scalp, then went to scrub up again. The anaesthetist was concentrating on adjusting his machine as a group of masked and gowned students arrived. There was a sudden hush, a stillness in the room, and then the anaesthetist nodded to Theodore. For a brief second his eyes met Zena's and held, then, his scalpel in his hand he bent over the table where Sami lay and the operation had begun.

Breathing shallowly and with a fluttering pulse Zena nevertheless responded smartly to his monosyllabic requests for instruments, naming each as she placed it decisively in his hand. As he probed and explored the brain tissue he explained to the onlookers what he was doing.

'There is a small splinter of bone embedded in here. An earlier gun-shot wound caused the trouble. I operated and removed a number of fragments but I was afraid something like this might happen. It is so minute it eluded me but it has recently been causing the patient a great deal of pain and occasional loss of balance and also of vision.'

He spoke automatically as his complete concentration was on what his hands were doing. Zena's mind flew to the previous night and much was explained now. Sami's drawn and pallid face, and the fact that he had not come to fetch her and his clumsiness when he dropped his cup as he missed the table. When he had leaned against the wall, his hands covering his face while she was questioning him, it was not because of his father's earlier hectoring, as she had imagined, but because he was in pain. If she had not been so full of herself and her own problems she would surely have suspected that something was seriously wrong with him. Maybe he had been wanting to tell her, to ask her advice, but she had not given him the opportunity; all she had done was to add to his pain by her persistence even though he had begged her to stop asking him questions. May I be forgiven, she prayed silently, and please give Theodore the skill to make the operation a success.

Under the heat and brilliance of the lights she watched Theodore's fingers moving so delicately that her own body prickled with nerves, and a pulse beat in her throat threatening her with sickness. The young nurse wiped the sweat from Theodore's forehead every few minutes and Zena thought that his back must be aching intolerably as he bent over the patient hour after hour, yet he seemed completely immersed in his task and his hands never faltered.

There was no sound now, save for the clink of metal, the hiss from the anaesthetic machine, and breathing. Theodore's voice suddenly sounded loud as he asked: 'How is he?'

The anaesthetist nodded. 'He's doing all right at the moment.'

'I shall try micro-surgery. The splinter is possibly too small to be seen with the naked eye.'

The students moved in closer to get a better view as Zena wheeled the microscope into position.

A dreadful thought struck Zena. What if the operation was not a success? And strangely her fears at this moment were not so much for Sami as for Theodore who had threatened that he would do anything to stop her marrying Sami. She knew without any doubt whatsoever that his personal feelings would not encroach on his professionalism, but surely he would always feel guilty and wonder whether he had in fact done his utmost for the patient if things went wrong? Please help him to make it a success, she prayed again.

As she watched the two men it seemed they were robots. Surely it was impossible for one human being to suffer his brain being probed for so long, and for the other to be so arduously engaged in doing so? Her attention was arrested suddenly by the anaesthetist. He made a movement towards Sami, then looked across at Theodore in concern. He opened his mouth to speak but at that moment Theodore said with immense satisfaction: 'Got it!' He peered at the tiny dot of bone and held it for the others to see. 'That's the little rogue. It doesn't look lethal, does it? But never be fooled by lack of size. It can do a hell of a lot of mischief. Right.' He turned to a doctor who was standing nearby. 'Will you close up, please?'

'As quickly as you can,' the anaesthetist said warningly.

A nurse busied herself at the trolley threading skin needles with nylon sutures, then put the needle-holder in the doctor's hand. Zena and Theodore took off their theatre clothes and threw them in the bin. He flexed the muscles of his neck and arms. 'Now for a cup of coffee. Are you coming, nurse?'

Zena gave a sigh of weariness. 'No, I must get back to the ward, we are short-staffed and one of the nurses should go off duty.'

'Can't it wait for as long as it takes to drink a cup of coffee?'

She shook her head. 'Better not; I have some patients due back from theatre and I should be there.' She began to walk away, knowing that she could not at this moment face the emotional stress of being alone with him. She turned back and with trembling lips said, 'I . . . I am so glad it went well. Thank you . . . thank you very much.' Her eyes were misty with unshed tears so she could not see the expression on his face, a mixture of anger and sorrow as he strode away.

Back in her ward three of the four patients who had returned from theatre had regained consciousness and were now sleeping. The fourth, who had had a gastrectomy, was complaining of feeling cold. Zena checked her temperature and blood pressure then switched on an electric blanket and arranged another over her feet.

'Nurse Shah,' she said, 'Thank you for staying on, I will take over now. Have you anything to report?'

She and Nurse Levinson continued with the medicine round then brought in bowls of water and tooth mugs for the bed-ridden patients. At the same time she was constantly hurrying back to the office to answer the telephone, chiefly enquiries from the patients' relatives as to their condition. By the time she had made up her report to hand over to the night staff she was completely exhausted, yet thankful that she had no time to think of anything but her work.

Wearily she crossed the courtyard to her bungalow. All she wanted was a snack, but it was too much effort to go to the canteen. After her third cup of coffee she felt somewhat restored and able to think back over the events of the day. She was deeply thankful that Theodore had found the splinter of bone. Although there had been no mention made of Sami's sight being affected she knew he would have believed it to be a possibility. She remembered his fear of that after the previous operation; how he had confessed his fears to no one but her. Was she, this time, going to withhold the support he had so valued? Surely she couldn't. And yet, equally surely, if she went to him she would be starting up their relationship anew. Her heart twisted with pain when she thought of all the times she could have chosen to tell Sami her decision, yet had picked the worst possible moment. Tears misted her eyes. She had to go to him and give him the comfort she knew he would crave. And if that meant that she would marry him, what then? Would it be right to marry out of pity? Yet it would not be pity alone for she did love him. He was kind and considerate and she could not repay that by staying away from him now.

She dragged herself to her feet and went to the bathroom to freshen up. She saw herself in the mirror and gave an exclamation of distaste. She looked a wreck, with shadows like bruises under her eyes and no vestige of colour in her cheeks. Like a robot she went out of her bungalow, closed the door and made her way to the hospital. As she waited for the lift to take her to the right floor she wondered numbly why she had ever worried what decision to make about her future, for now she believed it was all written in her stars; that events would carry her to whatever future was destined for her, and it was possible she would marry Sami regardless of what she had told him.

When she stepped out of the lift she walked mechani-

cally to the doors at the end of the corridor, passing
people whom she may or may not have known, disregarding them, until all of a sudden her stomach muscles
tightened and shivers ran down her spine. Overflowing
from a private room, looking like an eagle in his cream
dishdasha was Abu Sami and many of the men whom she
had seen last night at his house. She sped across to the
sister's office and knocked frantically on the door. An
offended voice bade her enter.

'Is there a fire, nurse? Is some patient haemorrhageing?' the Sister asked with a frown.

Her sarcasm was wasted on Zena. 'How is Mr Gharbally?' she asked, the words coming up to her throat like
sandpaper.

The sister's voice was coolly unconcerned. 'Mr Gharbally has not yet come around from the anaesthetic.
Why do you ask?'

'I assisted at the operation. And . . . and I know his
family.' She looked anxiously at the sister. 'Why has his
father been called for?'

'Called for?' She raised her eyebrows. 'He is here
together with many relations.'

'Why have they come?' Zena's voice cracked with
frustration.

The sister looked at her unsmilingly. 'How long have
you been in this country, nurse?'

Zena shook her head with an impatient frown. 'A few
weeks. Why?'

'Then possibly you do not know the Kuwaiti custom.
A close member of the family and relatives and friends
are always present when a patient wakes up from an
anaesthetic. It cheers them immensely to see family
faces and to know that the people they love are at
hand.'

A dull weight which had lain so heavily on Zena now
rolled away, leaving her with a feeling of immense relief.
Now she understood. It was because he had been in
England, a foreign country where none of his own
people could visit him that he had been so dependent on

her and grateful for her own comfort. Here, in Kuwait, he did not need her; he had his father.

On feet that were light now she walked from the office and back to the lift. She pressed the bell and as she waited there was a smile on her face. The gates opened and she stood aside to allow the passengers out.

'Oh . . . hello,' she said, startled at seeing Theodore. He gave her a cool nod of recognition, then joined by his followers made his way to the ward.

Her legs felt heavy again as she returned to her bungalow. Theodore's manner told her quite plainly that he had no interest in her at all, and although it was no news to her it made something inside her ache unbearably.

Now, without any more hesitation she must ask to be released from her contract. She went to her drawer and took out a writing pad, then sat at the table sucking her pen. The hospital authorities would not be pleased at her request, as she had been here for so short a time. She must say 'for personal and family reasons.' They could hardly argue with that. One of her parents might be seriously ill. After several abortive attempts she completed the letter to her satisfaction and placed it in an envelope which she addressed and sealed. Then, before she could change her mind and start wavering again, she took it across to the hospital and dropped it in the letter box.

As it fell from her fingers she had a feeling of panic and longed to get it back, and thought that if she came over early in the morning when the box was being emptied she could retrieve it, just to give herself longer to think about it. With that intention in mind she slowly crossed the courtyard. As she reached her door she saw Theodore approaching. She waited eagerly, but he turned in the direction of Beryl's bungalow. With a sigh she knew she had done the right thing in sending the letter, and had no intention of attempting to get it back.

CHAPTER TWELVE

THE next morning Zena went immediately to the men's surgical ward, anxious to know how Sami was progressing. She saw the sister approaching and, having no wish to speak with her again, went into the kitchen until she had passed. A nurse was in there, busy at the sink.

'Who are you? What do you want?' she asked with a foreign accent.

Zena gave a swift, placating smile. 'I know I should not be here, but please can you tell me how Mr Gharbally is doing? He had a brain op. yesterday.'

'He is all right. Why? Do you know him?'

'I . . . yes I do. And I was on theatre duty when Mr Smythe operated.'

'Ah yes, he is doing quite well. You would like to see him?'

Zena reluctantly shook her head. 'No . . . I . . . he hasn't . . . has he asked for anyone, do you know?'

The nurse shrugged her narrow shoulders. 'I do not know. He had many, many relations and friends with him. Such a commotion they make!'

'Commotion?' Zena knew the men had laughed and talked loudly at the party but surely they would not behave that way here?

The nurse laughed merrily. 'Yes they all make the oo's and aaah's, they do it to help him. You know?'

Zena thanked her and made her way to her own ward. As soon as she reached the corridor she knew that Beryl had returned. Whatever illness she had suffered, it had not impaired her voice. Zena tapped on the door and walked in.

'I hope you're feeling better,' she said.

To her surprise Beryl gave her a friendly smile. 'Yes thanks, I'm over it now, but it's a shocking thing when you've got it. I thought it must be something I ate at Theodore's party but apparently it was a virus and several of the staff have been down with it.'

They went through the charts together and discussed the happenings of the last few days and the condition of the patients. As she turned to leave the office Zena swung around and looked Beryl straight in the face. 'Mrs Ussher has been discharged. Her husband brought in several tubs of flowering plants. I think it was his way of apologising for the fuss his wife made about her earrings. I was relieved to know she had not lost them after all. Do you realise you forgot to tell me that?'

Beryl fiddled with some papers on her desk and said vaguely, 'Didn't I tell you? I expect I thought she'd told you herself.'

Zena felt unable to reply. She had no wish to get into an argument about it; all she wanted was to get away from the hospital and Kuwait as quickly as she could. She wondered how long it would be before she was sitting in the aeroplane on her way to Heathrow. She hoped the authorities would not withhold permission until they found a replacement nurse, for, despite the excellent working conditions, it was still difficult to get suitable staff.

It was a minor ops. day and she was kept busy with patients going to and coming from the theatre, so she had no time to think of Sami. But when she went off duty she stood undecided what to do. She pictured him looking up expectantly whenever his door opened maybe hoping it would be her, and she ached to go to him, but reluctantly decided against it. The thought of eating in the canteen did not tempt her so she went to her bungalow. After a long cool shower she put on a cream jersey silk house-coat and towelled her hair dry so that when she brushed it out it was like apricot candy-floss. She settled down to read and had a pot of coffee on the table beside her. When the doorbell rang she read hastily to the end of the paragraph, skipping words. Then, with her mind still on the story she padded bare-foot to the door, clutching her house-coat around her.

It was Theodore who stood there and she saw with dismay the hardness of his eyes, their pupils like pin-points. She gasped and instinctively made a move to shut the door, but he brushed her aside with an abrupt gesture and entered. She said with her professional air of authority, 'You have no right to force your way in here, you have not been invited.'

He ignored her remark and slapped a sheet of paper on the table. With a sickening jolt of dismay she recognised it as her own letter. She had realised that Theodore would be told of her request for the cancellation of her contract, but at no time had she imagined that her letter would be passed to him for him to deal with. PERMISSION REFUSED had been scrawled across it in thick black ink, and her heart sank.

His long thin index finger pointed disdainfully at the letter. 'And what is the meaning of this?' he demanded.

With a spurt of annoyance she said, 'I'm sorry, I thought I made it clear.' She leaned over and pretended to read it. 'Yes. I have asked to be released from my contract.'

A muscle twitched in his jaw as he stared at her for several long seconds. 'You agreed to come out here for a year, and now after only a few weeks you expect to be released from that contract. Is that the position?'

She looked at him coolly. 'Circumstances can change, you know,' she said.

'You have used the hospital for your own ends. You decided it was a good way to come out here to see your . . . lover . . . and have all your expenses paid. And I suppose you think that was very clever,' he said, his voice rasping.

Zena's hand flew to her mouth. 'Oh dear, I'm sorry, I never thought of it like that. Of course it . . . but I will pay back my fare and whatever else I owe if only I can be released,' she said.

She followed his eyes which were gazing down at her

body, and to her acute embarrassment she saw that her slippery silk house-coat had fallen apart. The colour flooded her cheeks as she drew the material together. 'I . . . I'm sorry,' she gasped.

A steely glint kindled in his eyes. 'Please don't trouble to apologise; I see such sights daily as you well know. You can rest assured that I am quite immune to your—er—womanly charms,' he drawled.

Her eyes smouldered with blue fire. 'Oh . . . you . . . I hate you!' she retorted.

His eyebrows went up slightly. 'Yes, I am well aware that you do, you have frequently told me so. However, we are not discussing your feelings for me. This is the matter in hand.' He tapped the offending letter again.

'So what more do you want me to do? Go down on my knees? I have asked to be released and have said I am willing to refund any money that is considered necessary.'

'So you have. It is quite a considerable sum of money . . . You will no doubt get it from your lover,' he said nastily.

'Please don't call him that,' Zena fumed. 'He is not my lover!'

'Really?' He spoke with quiet mockery. 'Are we expected then to await the refund until he is your husband?' His eyes narrowed. 'Or maybe we won't have so long to wait; perhaps it will be the price he is willing to pay for you.'

'How dare you!' Hurt beyond endurance by his insulting insinuations she seemed about to attack him, but he grabbed her arms, lifted her from the floor and flung her on to the settee. Then he knelt over her, his eyes glittering with anger. She saw the rippling muscles of his arms, felt the hardness of his body on hers and struggled to get her breath as her heart-beats threatened to choke her. Her face was but inches from his, her house-coat had fallen open again and she lay unclad and vulnerable beneath him.

'Are you aware,' he said threateningly, 'that I can stop

this marriage that you are so set on? In two minutes flat I can ensure that Gharbally would run a mile before he married you?'

Zena struggled frantically to get away from him but his legs straddled her so that she was imprisoned. 'I . . . I . . .' she stammered.

'Did you know that it is mandatory for a bride to be a virgin according to his customs?' he persisted, his weight heavy upon her.

Her eyes widened with indignation. 'Who said I wasn't?' she demanded.

'At the moment perhaps you are,' he said meaningfully.

Her breath exhaled in a loud gasp. 'Let me go!'

'I warned you that I would not tolerate you marrying this Gharbally fellow and I intend to do everything in my power to prevent it. Maybe not this . . . at the moment . . .' He jerked his head towards her body to show his meaning, then slowly moved away from her.

Zena was appalled at the treachery of her body for it ached for him to return to her, every sense yearned for his closeness, wanted his kisses, longed for . . . him. She scrambled to a sitting position, holding her house-coat together again.

He raised an ironic eyebrow. 'Rather a question of locking the stable door, don't you think?' He walked over to the wall and stood leaning against it. 'As you will realise your request for release is refused. By me. You will stay here at the hospital for the full year. I warn you there will be no question of you hoping to get out of it by marrying Gharbally, or even thinking you can marry him and work here as well, because his family would not permit it any more than I would. Make no mistake about that.'

She covered her face with her hands at the thought of the unhappy months ahead. 'But . . . but I am not happy here, can't you understand?' she asked, close to tears.

'You are a damned sight happier than you would be

married to Gharbally, believe me. No Zena,' he said and
the way he spoke her name was as if he had taken it and
polished it so that it seemed very precious, 'I hope that
by the end of the year you will have come to your senses,
realised how different it is out here, and exactly what
being married to him would entail. It will give you time
to get over your infatuation.' His voice lowered and
became tender. 'It is for your own good. I want you to be
happy.'

His change of manner, his sudden gentleness and
apparent concern for her took Zena unawares, melting
her anger and making her anxious that he should know
the truth. 'I . . . I asked for my contract to be cancelled
so that . . . so that I could return to England.'

He took a step towards her. 'You mean there really
are family reasons for your request to leave?'

She hesitated, tempted to lie, but she shook her head.
'Personal reasons. I said family and personal reasons, so
it is almost true. I . . . oh Theodore, I can't stay on out
here, hating it, with nobody . . . nobody at all. I . . .'
She was reluctant to tell him but the words came unbid-
den to her lips. 'I . . . I have told Sami that I can't marry
him.'

There was complete silence for a moment, then when
he spoke his voice was slow and thoughtful. 'You went to
his house the night before he was brought in here . . . I
saw the car call for you. Then, yesterday you went to the
ward to see him. So when did you tell him?'

She ran her fingers distractedly through her hair. 'I
. . . I told him the night I went to his house. And since
then I have felt so cruel. I know now that he was in great
pain and yet I told him. I wish from the bottom of my
heart that I hadn't said anything . . . you can't imagine
how dreadful I feel about it.' Her head drooped.

He said accusingly, 'And then you went to his ward to
tell him you had made a mistake and would marry him
after all, is that it? You would marry him out of pity?'

She shook her head. 'No, I didn't do that.'

'I know you didn't because he was still under the

anaesthetic. But that was your intention, wasn't it?' he persisted.

'No, no it wasn't, I just wanted to make sure he had not been asking for me . . .'

'And if he had been . . . ?'

'I . . . I don't know,' she said miserably.

The ticking of the little carriage clock sounded loud in the quiet room. Then Theodore said softly, 'You really love him, don't you?'

Zena looked at him, wide-eyed and desperate. 'I can't help I . . . loving him he is so kind and considerate . . . and gentle.'

There was a glint in Theodore's eyes. 'In fact the complete opposite to me.'

Her thick lashes cast shadows on her cheeks. She made no answer.

'If he has all those qualities, what prompted you to refuse him?'

Her voice was strangled. 'Because it wouldn't work; our customs are so different. All the things you told me are true.'

He sat beside her on the settee, his arm along its back. He studied her curiously, a strange glint in his eyes. 'Do you believe everything I tell you?'

She thought for a moment, then slowly nodded her head. 'Yes, I think I do.'

He twisted a tress of her hair around his finger and asked casually, 'Would you believe me if I told you I loved you?'

She covered her face with her hands and shuddered convulsively. 'I think you are the cruellest man I have ever known; everything you say is meant to hurt me,' she said, half sobbing.

He removed his arm from the settee and slid it around her, imprisoning her with the other. She could feel the strong thud of his heart-beat through the thinness of her wrap. 'Haven't you heard that a man always hurts the thing he loves? I agree that I am the opposite of your precious Sami. I am cruel, inconsiderate and can be

very, very rough, but I love you, and because of some
chemical reaction I want you very badly. Are you going
to marry me or will I have to try and get you some other
way?' He held her face between his hands but as she
looked into his eyes they were unreadable. She did not
know whether he was teasing, or whether he would
throw her answer back in her face. She only knew that if
she did not take him up on his offer immediately she
would regret it for the rest of her life, indeed life would
not be worth living.

'I will marry you,' she said simply.

The words had scarcely left her lips before they were
silenced by his firm mouth. Flattened beneath him by the
weight of his body she felt as though her bones were fluid
and the blood that coursed through her veins was
alive with electricity. His knowledgeable, delicate
surgeon's hands moved expertly over her body sending
tremors of delight in their wake. When the ecstasy was
almost too much to bear he moved reluctantly away
from her.

'I want you more than I ever wanted anything,' he said
hoarsely, 'but I intend to wait until you are my bride. In
that one thing I am like Sami.'

Zena pulled his face down against hers again. 'Do you
think that in two minutes flat I could get you to change
your mind?'

'So you are brazen as well as bossy, disobedient and
tantalising,' he said, punctuating his remarks with kisses
on her forehead and eyes and the tip of her nose.
'Between us we've got all the faults in the book. But at
least I will be able to keep you in order. I'll beat you
regularly,' he told her cheerfully, but when she looked
into his eyes they were full of love and tenderness.

'Bully! You think you can do what you like just
because . . .'

'Because I'm bigger than you are,' he laughed, remembering. He hugged her roughly to his side. 'Let me
see. We will get married . . . when? Next week? Next
month? There's room in my bungalow for two.'

Happiness went through her like a flame to be replaced by a sudden coldness. 'What about Beryl?' she faltered.

His eyes narrowed. 'What about her?'

'She . . . you . . . she is in love with you, you know that? I thought you loved her too.' Her face took on a worried look.

He ran his fingers through his hair. 'We're just good pals. We always have been ever since we trained together. I respect her work as she does mine.'

In her mind was the picture of Beryl and Theodore laughing together, their arms entwined. She shook her head dubiously. 'It looked like more than that to me,' she said.

He crossed the room and stared out of the window. 'It goes back some time, Zena; I didn't really want to speak of it now. But . . .' He shrugged his shoulders. 'I had a brother . . . Jonathan . . . he was two years younger than me but we were always very close. He was very popular, full of fun and laughter. He met Beryl at one of our hospital functions and straightaway they hit it off. They made a super couple. They had fixed the date of their wedding . . .' His voice died away and there was silence in the room. When he continued speaking his voice was so low that she had to strain to hear. 'I was always scared that something would happen . . . and it did. It was at Brands Hatch . . . he was a racing driver . . . he got smashed up.'

Zena gave a small exclamation of distress but he ignored it. 'Beryl was great. She said it wouldn't make any difference to their plans . . . although of course the date had to be postponed.' He cleared his throat. 'Then . . . before another date could be fixed he took an overdose.'

Zena walked over to join him and laid her hand on his arm. 'I'm very sorry,' she said.

'It was a blow to us all. But knowing Jonathan I realise it was the way he wanted it. Not only was his face terribly burnt but he was paralysed from the waist down. 'So,' he took a deep breath, 'Beryl and I mourned his loss together.'

And then Beryl transferred her love to you, Zena thought. It was understandable.

'Have . . . have you ever considered marrying her?' Zena's voice wobbled.

A look of uncertainty clouded his eyes. 'I wouldn't be telling the truth if I said the idea had not crossed my mind. We have so much in common and I am very fond of her . . . partly because of what we have suffered together. But I think I always knew that what I felt for her was pity more than love, and pity is no basis for marriage.' He braced his shoulders. 'But no more talk of Beryl; this moment is for us. A very special moment.'

She was eager to take his mind off his sad memories and asked with a smile, 'So what do you feel for me, Theodore?'

He laid his finger on the tip of her nose. 'Desire,' he said simply.

She squinted down at it. 'Desire is just physical attraction, and that is no basis for marriage for it will pass,' she warned him.

He stared down at her with a look of deep devotion and warmth in his eyes. 'No, my darling, it is not just desire, but how can I describe what I feel? How can I explain the physical pain I felt at the mere idea of you marrying somebody else? Of knowing you belonged to another man? Of my longing to hold you and touch your hair and your skin? I have been through hell in the last few weeks. And it is so incredible. I have always considered so carefully before I did or said or decided on anything, and yet when I first saw you I fell in love with you. It doesn't make sense.'

'It does to me,' Zena said, weak with happiness, 'for I felt the same way about you.'

'But you said you hated me,' he protested.

She sighed. 'I know. In a funny sort of way I did that too.' She wound her arms around his neck.

His lips were warm and tender against her mouth.

When at last she was able, she said, 'It will be so lovely not having to work in the hospital.'

He stared up at the ceiling, apparently deep in thought. Then he said: 'I think you must go on working there, you would be bored stiff with nothing to occupy your time. I have got to see this year out; I am not retracting on my contract. Besides,' the corners of his mouth twitched, 'it will do you no harm at all to be bossed around a bit, it will make you into a docile wife.'

Incensed, Zena drew away from him, beating her hands on his chest, but he grasped them and had her at his mercy again with the fierce pressure of his body against hers. Then the knowledge came to her that whatever he decreed, whatever he said she must do, she would gladly obey. Was this what Sami had meant when he described love?

'Don't worry, my darling,' Theodore whispered in her ear, 'as my wife you will be the most cherished woman in the world and I shall make sure that you are happy, now and always.'